THE PACK'S DRAGON 1

RACHEL D. ADAMS
&
DAWN MCCLELLAN

The Pack's Dragon

Digital ISBN: 978-1-958442-02-9

Paperback ISBN: 9781958442036

Cover Art by Donika Mishineva, Formatting design by Rachel D. Adams, Thank you to our Beta Readers: Sam Wicker and Tisha

WTC Creatives

500 Westover Dr #16238

Sanford, NC 27330

www.racheldadams.com

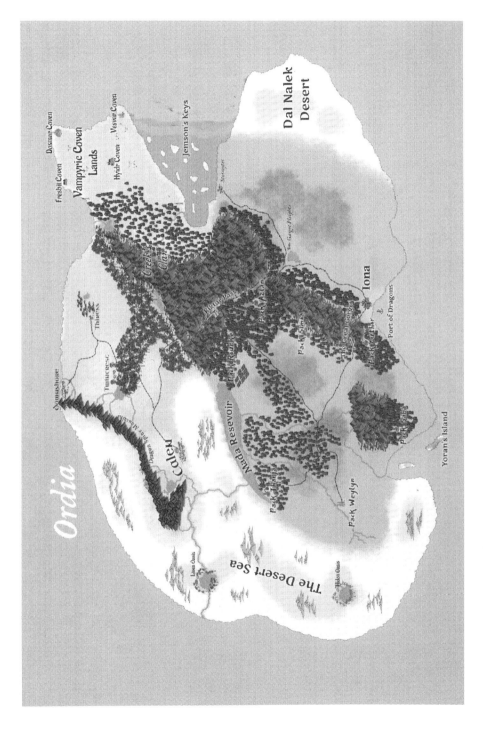

CONTENTS

CHAPTER ONE

BATTLES THAT RAGE

KIERAN WAS IN THE middle of blood lust. A creature half dire wolf and half man, he stood tall as two elves on top of each other. This was the last thing many elves saw before they met their makers. And Kieran's bloodline was royal; Alpha. That meant he had something to prove, and he had a pack to fight for. Fight, he did.

The big gray pack leader jumped to gain height and then landed in the middle of some elves, who were giving his warriors a hard time. Some scattered, and others got tossed around. One unfortunate got snatched by the head. With the snap of his neck, his long life ended.

The old Alpha had often wondered why it had taken so long for his kind to get free of these creatures. Sure, they lived a long time, and sure, they had magic on their side. But they were more fragile than most lycan - and they damn sure couldn't heal. The sound of battle was all around him. When Kieran looked to the side, he could see Devon, his son, deep in battle as well.

Devon was the same as him: big, blonde, and bestial. They were both in their hybrid forms and they were making good use of the strength, the claws, the size, and the teeth. Not to mention, their bodies healed from wounds quickly. The younger lycan grabbed an attacker by the shoulder with his teeth. The air filled with the sounds of ripping flesh and screams when the elf got tossed through the air. He lunged forward, taking hits, but moving so that those injuries were superficial as possible and healing quickly.

Kieran's other son, a berserker-like ball of black-furred fury, followed his father. He bounced over elf after elf, slicing their faces and eyes and taking out as many as possible. Gareth's bright blue eyes shimmered as he went wild on all the elves that he could get to. He was smaller built than the others, but that just meant he could move a lot quicker and get in more attacks. He was just as lithe as the elves he fought; sometimes quicker. Using his lupine instincts only made him more lethal.

Kieran stepped on an elf he had just downed and raised his head to howl a signal for his men. Before anyone could attack, another dark-furred lycan pulled up in front of him, ready to bat away anybody that wanted to take the chance. He was not of the royal family, but he was a loyal lycan in the command of Kieran.

"Argoth, back!" Kieran ordered as his form shrunk slightly into the more human version of himself. He held up a still slightly clawed hand just in time to catch an elvish arrow before it hit Argoth in the head. Kieran let his muzzle expand again so he could bite off the head of the arrow and yanked the shaft out of his palm. He began healing immediately.

Argoth and Kieran backed up, and so did the rest of their warriors. Believing they were gaining the advantage, elves continued fighting and moving forward. There was a whistling sound of thousands of arrows flying over their heads to bury in the bodies of elves. The rest of the lycan got out of the way as quickly as they could. Elves were making the most of what they had, trying to keep the line moving in the direction they needed it to move. The screams of their brethren filled their ears. Soon, the sound of a great horn told the lycan that the elves planned to retreat.

However, Kieran's scouts were howling, barking news through the ranks, growling in their fury. Elves were lining the cliffs and normally would have had the advantage here. They'd already been losing their own barrages of arrows during this battle, sure, but what they were doing now wasn't about that.

The elves began launching ropes from one side of the chasm to the other, forming an intricate net. Expectation and planning might buy confidence, but did it buy them safety?

Argoth watched Devon and Gareth back off from the fighting to make their way to the big alpha. Kieran began growling orders to those around him. But his eyes seemed fixed on the horizon. Argoth tugged him backward.

Those amber eyes focused somewhere other than the flurry of movement right before him. In his mind, he could feel the wind in the late afternoon skies. He could smell the ozone, and see the battle from far, far higher than he was. These were things his mind was seeing, feeling, and smelling...

The Elven preparation was to halt those magnificent creatures swimming through the clouds. But Kieran had a bond with both. He warned them. The roars and growls from the retreating lycan got washed out and overwhelmed by a deeper roar that came from the clouds up above.

The clouds tumbled downward as if part of a waterfall as two dragons breached. One was dark and the other light. The dragons matched in size and ferocity. They stopped moving their wings and simply dove into a parallel glide over the sides of the gorge the battle was being fought in. The dragons strafed liquid fire along each side of the large crevasse. Lines that zig-zagged over the top to form a net burned and fell to the ground. The flames melted the elves that had set the lines where they stood.

The dragons made a great U in the far sky, high above before one came down to strafe the elves inside the walls of this deadly canyon. The other, the black and maroon scaled beast, wrapped his claw around the Elven leader and his mount. He lifted their commander and dropped him from the clouds to land among the burning thousands.

Kieran shook his head to come back out of what he could sense through the light bond he shared with those dragons. Argoth, his second, still tugged him backward, away from the intense heat they could all feel. The alpha growled and shook off the scout. Argoth growled right back, but that was as far as it went. He turned to find his own son, Derek, at his side. All five warriors in this group witnessed the inferno and defeat of their enemy.

Afterward, the Alpha of Pack Weylyn watched his warriors take in surrendering elves. Devon came back to him from the ranks. He and the dark-furred Gareth both shifted in front of their father to look more like what a standard human might look. Their hair was a bloody, matted mess.

"Only a few of our pack are down. We'll know more when the flames have died. As always, Senias and Inea have done well to keep the casualties to the side of the elves. I think...maybe this was the finish." Devon turned back to the mess. Then, all five of them looked up as both dragons swooped back across the fiery scene, orange flames beginning to meld with the dramatic sky of sunset.

"The elves of Calan will never hold our people as slaves, again," Kieran huffed air from his nose and howled again. This time, there were answering howls from all over the battleground.

CHAPTER TWO

RISE AND SHINE

IT HAD BEEN TWO days of clean-up and finally, Pack Weylyn had time to settle down. A lot of the warriors went home. Others flocked to the local towns and onward to Iona - the great city of the East, near the main portal that led to the world on the other side.

The city was a gambling town, and Kieran wanted no part of it for now. He felt like his own control was loose these days. He didn't need temptations more than he already came across. So, he had made sure that his most trusted warriors and his dragons had suitable rooms at an inn and tavern called Fanny's Man. It was in a town between the last battle and their packlands to the southwest. They all needed the rest, and he needed the time to decide on plans of action. Just because they won a deciding battle didn't mean the work was done.

Walking from his own room, the older lycan tossed a pack over one shoulder while moving his fingers through the still damp, blonde, and silver hair on the side of his head. The other side had fresh braids, beads clinking on one another. He had so many. One for the pack, one for his mate, one for each pup, one for each major war and battle worth remembering...

He walked down the hall to the stairs. Kieran hated having to use the mind to speak to get his dragons up out of bed. Especially Senias. He swore that dragon loved trying to shock them every time he got a chance.

~ If I hafta come in after yer ass, there won't be much left, Scales, ~ Kieran warned the dragon. They'd been friends and fighting comrades for several years now. He'd gotten used to this. As Kieran made his way to the bottom of the stairs, the lycan alpha motioned for the barkeep to come over to the table he was heading for so he could settle up.

~ You're no fun. Can't even sleep in? ~ Senias rolled over and immediately off the bed with a solid thump! The hung-over man groaned as he put his arm over his eyes. Daylight was not on the menu. Kieran could probably feel every bit of the aggravation through their bond.

~ Mornin's already gone. Get up before half the damn day's gone. You have slept in, ya sot. Now get movin' ~ Kieran shook his head, his shaggy blonde hair clacking where it was braided and hung loose for the time.

UPSTAIRS IN THE ROOM, Senias lifted himself slowly from the floorboards. Sometimes, he felt like he'd made a mistake in teaching Kieran the way to use mind-speak.

"What?" the voice behind him up in the bed asked. It was a rough sound. The common tongue wasn't something this lycan was used to speaking. But his voice was attractive, just the same. And the dragon had enjoyed making him use it.

"Gotta get going, I'm afraid. But the room's paid 'til nightfall. Enjoy it as much as I enjoyed you."

The draconic male chuckled before stepping over to the basin for a good scrub. He always carried exotic scents from the other side with him to help with masking the smell of good sex and sweat. When you traveled with lycan, who had the best noses around, you didn't need them knowing all your business.

"Good. I don't need ta be showing' face downstairs, anyway." The man stretched and then turned over. He didn't bother with covers.

Senias chuckled. There was no need for the fella to be bashful now. So, he shrugged and went back to his cleaning up and getting dressed. He had touched and tasted every bit of that body the night before, and yet, he wasn't actually sure of the warrior's name.

Did it matter?

WHEN HE CAME DOWN the steps, Senias was still strapping on his sword belt. His bag was over his shoulder, and he was scanning the common room for his other compatriots. He spoke clearly to Devon. "Your old man is a hard-assed slave driver."

"Your mouth won't get him riled if he ain't here ta hear it, Scales. Our Alpha just stepped out. You have impeccable fuckin' timing," Argoth countered while he looked over a letter he'd received at the last post grab. The dark-haired lycan had a secret admirer, or his own mate was just good at keeping him enthralled. That was for sure.

Looking up from his mug of ale, the dirty blonde lycan chuckled. Devon nudged his dark-haired friend. "Hear that, Argoth? He's finally starting' to understand, my ole man." With a shake of his head, Devon picked up the bread on the table and broke it for sharing while they waited for the rest of their food. Senias sat across the table from the other two and sighed loudly.

"Glad we didn't have to drag you from bed this time." Argoth folded the letter to put away. "Your bedmates never really appreciate that." Blue eyes sparkled as they lifted to the dragon, who was joining them.

"Bedmates?" there was a rough shake of Dev's dirty blonde hair and a rumble from his chest, "I never know what or who he'll have in that bed with him or how many. Let's just say more times than not, I'd just as soon let him roll out on his own." He sighed and finished his ale before wiping the dregs from his short bristle of a beard.

"Smart wolf, there," Senias flicked his tongue in a perverted manner.

After a good, deep laugh, Argoth held a fresh mug out to the new arrival. "Does this mean you'll be joining' us for the next battle, Senias?"

Taking the mug, he swirled the liquid around inside of it and then took a drink. Snarling his nose up at it, Sen put the stuff back on the table.

"Not like I'm a surprise anymore. They all know Pack Weylyn has dragons on their side. And those damned elves who keep hold of slaves and lycan lands need to just give up, if you ask me," the dragon looked at the other two warriors.

"I told ya, Sen, don't care about the petty squabbles these days, right? He prefers to hold back and join the big battles like the one coming up." Golden eyes shifted to the dragon. "Will ya be ridin'out with us or comin' in with the second wave?"

"He'll be in the second wave." Kieran was walking back by, looking at the door and then back to the stairs.

"Shouldn't he get to decide his fate, ole man?" Devon asked his father, noting the way their Alpha was looking around expectantly.

"He signed up for this and so did his mate. They do as I need them ta do, son. You know that." Kieran rumbled as he asked, "Where are Gareth and Derek? I thought they were joining' us here with you and the others."

"I'm sure Gareth'll be here shortly," Senias cleared his throat before leaving the table for the nearby end of the bar. "Distilled liquor, barrel mash, or whatever you call your whiskey here. I never know." The barkeep nodded and while he was getting the liquor, Sen grabbed one of the sweet rolls they had out. Gar was Devon's brother and the only one he could vouch for. After all, he knew why the young man was late.

"I'm here. Get yer knickers out of a knot," a young man with golden-blonde hair and eyes as blue as his Argoth's made his way toward the table from the front of the tavern.

Kieran gave Derek a death stare.

"Sir." Derek looked aside and made his way around Kieran, taking a wide berth. "Where to today? More scouting?"

Senias felt bad for the green ones. Derek and Gareth hadn't really experienced dangerous situations yet. They still got excited over the least little mission. Derek never knew where his duties fell. Sometimes he was to scout. Sometimes he was part of the initial troops. He never seemed to mind, but instead of traveling with anyone else, the kid always remained near his father and the rest of their primary group of warriors.

"Word is the Elven front slowed down. We've got a few days. And I've had reports of another slaver's camp movin' through the area. You know how I feel about them, so I thought you ought ta introduce yourselves. That'll give you and Gar some much-needed practice in a halfway-controlled environment." Kieran looked around, "That is if his highness wants ta show up today."

Devon couldn't help but chuckle.

Senias remained quiet. As if on cue, the other dragon appeared from the back hallway. The sun-kissed platinum-haired woman walked into the main hall. She was in her normal loose pants cinched at the ankle and shirt beneath her corset vest ensemble. Her weapons were on her side, though everyone knew what was dangerous about Inea wasn't a physical weapon, but the spells. Her eyes went to Kieran, and she smiled like the cat that ate the canary.

"Good morning?"

Kieran growled.

"Is it not a good morning?" The dragoness played coy before moving toward her partner at the bar. "Sen." The other dragon simply bowed his head to her and took the whiskey offered by the barkeep. He passed her a roll.

"Mornin' Inea, don't suppose you've seen my brother, have ya?" Devon chuckled.

"Maybe an hour ago, when I got up and left the room. I always let people sleep if they need it. I'm nothing if not polite," Inea's eyes sparkled.

"You romp around too much, I swear..." Kieran muttered.

"But we get the job done for you, right?" Senias pointed out, defending both him and his mate's fun. They had taken lovers left and right, both here and in their original world, so why would they feel ashamed of it? "Just because you lycan limit yourselves doesn't mean we have to."

With drinks and rolls in hand, the two dragons moved to join the rest at the table. When Gareth appeared a few moments later, he was pulling his shirt down over his young, lean-built form. His dark braids clicked together on the right side of his head as he adjusted his clothing. He said nothing as he moved past his father, their Alpha.

"Mornin' all, how'd the scouting' go?" Gareth took a seat beside Inea and rested his arm around her shoulders. Gareth lived on the Alpha's bad side. He'd become used to it, just as he'd become used to Devon defending him against their sire.

"Oh, that's sweet, but it's not necessary," she whispered to Gar. Inea knew he was doing it to show off and that wasn't appetizing to her likes at all. Inea took some dates and nuts from the bowl in front of her and began digging in without waiting.

Gareth withdrew his arm and seated himself properly while keeping his thoughts to himself.

"I was just telling' the others that we found some slavers. Dev and Argoth'll take you and Dare out to give 'em a proper lycan greetin'. Look around the place and see if they plan on coming into our territory. If they do, we'll shut them down without causing harm to the innocent. We need ta know who they got with 'em and how they set those tents up before that." Kieran was now finally taking his seat. He pulled a biscuit out of the basket and ladled gravy over it.

"Might need to have a plan before going..." Senias began.

"No dragons."

"Oh?" Senias had a brow raised and the alpha now had his full attention. "Why no dragons?"

"Time to put your mettle back up where it needs ta be." Kieran looked across at the two younger lycan. "Be careful of yer beasts around the slaves. They don't want ta be there. And ya both need ta brush up on being diplomats. Find out what the scoundrel knows about the elf and lycan movements."

"My beast is in its cage for now. I don't have a habit of spilling innocent blood." Gareth rumbled as he reached for a biscuit to bite into.

"They're having a bonfire tonight. Yer just going ta the festivities because they like having' good clients. I've dealt with Madron Regis before. His information is good for the money or favor. So be good clients." Kieran already had this formula down perfectly.

"So, we don't get to go to the party?" Inea asked. She looked from Kieran to Senias.

"I have something else for you to get into," Kieran pointed out before motioning for both to come with him. The dragoness sighed and handed the last date to Gareth, whose eyes brightened before he took the offered morsel.

Senias and Inea left the table and paused at the door while Kieran continued the conversation.

"Somebody needs to be chattin' up the leader of the caravan while the others get yer paws in and around what's going on amongst his men." Kieran surveyed the boys. "You'll need better clothes. Here," he tossed some gold on the table. "This filth and their slaves usually know everything that's been going on from the portals outward. Get the information and find out where they're headed next. If they get within two sniffs of our packlands, I want them taken down. But for now, we use 'em."

"You think the other dragons to the north might, you know... step in?" Derek asked.

"No, knucklehead." Kieran gave Derek a perturbed look. "The dragons of this world ain't my worry. But the elves on the northern side? Now that's my worry. They're gettin' way too close to our allied packlands. Those Calen elves that we've not been able to capture? They would've had to traipse close to or through both Rourke and Azlan packlands. That slaver and those in caravans like his? They pass through those areas. They'll know something."

Taking the gold, Devon tucked it away while standing.

"Which means Dare and I are going to be the royal escorts for the two princes here." Argoth squeezed Derek's shoulder. He grinned at the young man before winking. "Think you're up to it, son?"

"I'm as up to it as I could ever be up to anything," He shrugged. "I've been a royal guard a lot. It's nothing new, huh, Gar?"

"It's boring." Gareth wasn't one to pretend. "I'm certain we'll get the details that we need from the slavers. Is Pack Rourke preparing for any unexpected attacks that may be coming their way? Or are they leaving their security up to our Pack?" Gareth asked their father as he stood up beside Devon, who was preparing to head out.

"Don't look down yer nose at Pack Rourke. They took a big hit last time while protecting our borders. They saved our troops from the west side. We owe 'em. I don't doubt they have the spirit; I just wonder do they have all the power to put behind it. That's why the dragons are going ahead."

"It ain't just Rourke, we got help from Pack Simoa and Pack Azlan, too." Gareth watched his father. "Shouldn't the dragons visit each?"

"They will. They'll start in Simoa, then up to Azlan, then across to Rourke. Should take a couple of days. So, plenty of time ta find out any other information that comes along."

CHAPTER THREE

THE TRADE OF LIVES

THE NIGHT WAS COOL, close to the border between pine forests and the coast. The caravan had parked out near the beach instead of heading further into the city. Devon, Gareth, Argoth, and Derek had run most of the way from the last inn to get to the shore. This was now a casual encounter for Kieran Weylyn's sons and their guards. Less intimidation meant looser mouths. And there would be others from the city around as well, all to sample the wares and just enjoy the night with these travelers.

Of course, there was music and a huge bonfire made of local wood and driftwood alike. The sand was still warm from the light of the day when everything had begun.

"Looks like they started the party without us," Derek pointed out as they made their way. They had on the gear of sand travelers, light cloth with silk sashes, and goggles that hung on their sides. They wore no shoes, most lycan didn't.

"Shhh... remember your position," Argoth cautioned his son as he walked a pace behind the well-dressed forms of the princes of Pack Weylyn.

Devon was in dark green and brown while his brother sported his usual blues and blacks. They were the colorful ones of this group because they were royalty. This let the slavers and those around them know who to speak with about trade. They moved through the crowd and could feel the change in the atmosphere.

"Well, look who has graced us with their presence." Madron Regis was one of the shrewdest traders in the lands. His stature showed in his lack of worry about his own condition. Surrounded by luxury at all camps, he'd eaten the best food and rarely had to make a run for it. His physical countenance showed that. "I hope you've brought your coin or your promissory papers to my event, gentlemen. Pack Weylyn, I assume?" He saw Devon lift a hand, but before the wolf could say a thing, he tsked his tongue. "No worries. My deals are confidential and the others who might be round this event would like all to remain just as confidential. Not everyone is open about what they like to purchase, yes?"

"You know what we Weylyn like ta buy? There's no shame in that." Gareth pointed out. "Weapons and information are the only things we like. Keep your slaves."

"Servants, m'lord. They are servants, and you would purchase their limited servitude from me, nothing more." His fingers went together in a small triangle at his waist, a silent way of letting his guests know what he could get away with. "Perhaps the younger prince of a pup has not learned from his elder brother the ways of discretion when speaking of trade?"

"I ain't no pup..."

"I see you've gathered quite the lot this time, Regis." Devon followed the other man through the camp, poking his brother in the side when the slaver turned to lead them. He showed little interest in the revelers or the slaves, moving instead to the ringed-off area around the dancing and near the bonfire.

"Come, come! Let us enjoy some time here in the daze." Madron Regis was a merry older fellow with quite a wheeze. He wore silks of the lands, and they showed his salt and pepper hair, both on his head and his chest. There was a carpeted area surrounded by pillows instead of the hard benches that the others usually went for. The man even had a hookah set up. "What can I do for you?" he asked as he struggled to get his bulk down onto the pillows.

Derek remained near Gar and Argoth near Devon - all of them let Devon lead.

Gar was watching a lot of the ladies who were merry making with men that were obviously from the local villages and the cities surrounding this area. There were servants seeing that everyone got food and drink and...well, whatever else the master of the caravan allowed. They were all being entertained by the dancers most of all. Some were slaves that Regis would part with. One could tell by the blue wristbands they wore.

Devon's golden eyes moved over the servants, and he took a seat while motioning Gareth to do the same.

"Not sure you can do anything for me, but I thought I'd take a chance and see what you offer. My father wasn't keen on this visit, but I convinced him it might prove its worth. He didn't want to be bothered, so we came. Tell me, have I wasted my time?" His deep voice rumbled through the ending words, as the lycan often did when they were trying to get a point across. Devon thought nothing of the sound until he noticed it caused at least one dancer to stop in her tracks. His soft, amber-colored eyes paused on her.

The other dancers adorned her with pale colors because of her dark-toned skin. Her reddish hair was obviously curly but forced into a large braid, woven with pale-colored ribbons to match the skirt and midriff shirt she wore. Madron had gone all out and made sure all the servant women had semi-precious gems in their navels. Those and the glistening moisturizers that smelled exquisite on their skin added to their beauty. The others moved around her as she did something that was not normally allowed. She made eye contact with a freeborn.

"You're a Weylyn and so you want information. Isn't it always thus?" Regis took a nice draw from the tobacco and let the smoke slowly erupt from his lips.

"You have news?" While he spoke, Devon couldn't keep his gaze from shifting to take in the small gathering of marked men and women who walked by. They sought freedom by being purchased from the slavers. Unfortunately, he couldn't offer much to them. He detested the trade of freedom, but this world allowed it, no matter what he thought of it.

But Devon found himself caught by the dark beauty's gaze, and she seemed bold enough to hold it. He gave a partial grin in response before his brother nudged him back into the conversation.

"Pardon me, you were saying?"

"I said nothing, yet..." Madron chuckled. "You like what you see?" He was always ready to make a deal. "That one is special. She come from the other side, trained among vampires."

Argoth saw the slave move off quickly. She was gorgeous, that was for sure. But if you tangled with a slave, you had to pay for it. He hoped Devon remembered that. She wasn't an elf, so maybe they were good.

"Elves of the Ricktor Pass, tell me what you know." Devon was fighting back the temptation to go into the crowd and find the woman that had held his gaze. He had business to tend to above any other interests.

"Information on the elves, eh?" Regis sat forward and held out his hand. "You buy this as you would anything else. You know the price."

As Devon nodded at him, Argoth held out the coin bag.

Sitting back, the gold moving through his fingers and then disappearing, Madron cleared his throat. "You, Weylyn, need not worry. These elves, they have another target in mind. They're not dumb enough to go after the pack so strong, but they *do* move magic. I see that with my own sorry eyes. So be aware."

"They've had magic all this time and nothing's ever come of it," Devon pointed out.

"You've always made good defenses, outlasted them, and rumor has it you have dragons." Madron took another draw on his hookah. Before offering it to Gareth. The younger lycan took the nozzle for a nip.

"So, the dragons have kept us protected from magic?" Devon asked quietly, his eyes scanning the dancing slaves. He wanted to be sure no one was occupying the time of the beautiful one that had held his gaze.

"I've felt magic more'n once out there," Derek muttered before getting a scalding gaze from his father. He averted his own gaze to the ground quickly.

"Rourke don't have magic or dragons, Devon." Gareth wanted to be sure his older brother remembered that.

"Mmm..." Devon stood up and looked around. His eyes didn't stop moving around the tents and the smaller bonfire between. His brother passed the hookah pipe back to Regis and got up as well.

"Neither do the other packs that are between here and Calen up the pass. And that will be the only exit route for the elves still here. If you get my meaning." Regis took a deep breath. "But the elves of Calen, they retreat. We've seen such with our own eyes and can confirm."

"You just can't confirm if they'll try to strike the other packs as they leave." Devon moved his hand over his scraggly beard. "Maybe Gar's right. We need to go."

"Things, they will not change in a night's time. If the prince would like to sample, an arrangement can be made, yes?" Madron tempted.

Devon didn't like it when a stranger knew his mind. He had every intention of turning away and leaving. Gareth even read that in his positioning and movement. But then he saw her again. She turned in the dance away from another trader and back into the group of women before looking at their group and locking eyes with him. She even intrigued his inner wolf. But then, everyone was moving again, and he lost track of her.

"Dev, we need to get back," Gareth whispered.

"It's not an emergency, Gar. Besides, the dragons were supposed to make their way to the Rourke Packlands before we were to be done here. We've got time to enjoy."

The guards both wore surprised expressions. But they said nothing.

"If you're sure. You're in charge." Gareth shrugged. He turned toward the dancers, who were enjoying cavorting with the men they were looking to woo. "Maybe a dance or two wouldn't hurt, nothin'."

"Remember your control." Devon cautioned.

Argoth, who was behind Devon, chuckled and cautioned his best friend, "Seems you may need to remember your control as well, dear prince."

That earned the dark-haired lycan 'guard' a narrowed glare. But Devon followed their host to where the dancing and entertainment were going on. Of course, with their status, all four had women vying for their attention. While they coaxed the others into dancing, Devon kept alone.

"Prince, are you not going to join the others for the dancing?" Madron came back after checking on the rest of the festivities.

"They're all lovely, but not for me. The others are enjoying well enough." Devon waved a persistent Regis off.

"Your eyes, they search. Tell me you just don't see her? Eh?" Regis clapped the big lycan's shoulder. Devon cut a bit of glare over at the unsavory man, but he didn't answer. "Tell you what, I do you this favor and hope you and your family will one day see favor upon mine?" He smiled and leaned in close to the elder prince. "Her name it has not been spoken. She is stubborn. I would not sell her in 12 cities, despite her beauty. She is too smart for most. From the other side of the great portals." He laughed that low, wheezing laugh.

Devon stood up straight and cleared his throat. Pretending disinterest was difficult.

"Go to the main trail we have between tents. The opening of the second tent. Look inside. She will be there. Maybe you'll get lucky? Maybe she dance with you? I order her to dance with my clients otherwise." He walked back toward the crowd. "That one, she's too much trouble. I would part with her for a deal." His voice faded away into the music and crowd.

Derek was keeping an eye out, even while he was being led to dance alongside Gareth. He was on Gar duty... his dad always took Devon duty. So, when the heir to the Weylyn Pack turned and tried to scoot away from his handlers, Derek was ready to whistle to his father. But Argoth had it handled. He was soon falling into step, not far behind Devon.

"Your mind focuses on the wrong things this trip, my friend."

"Maybe. But if I don't find out, I'll drive myself crazy."

"Dancin' is one thing, Dev. If you want this gal, you'll have to pay for her. You'll be contributing to this trade. You know how wrong that is?"

"Look, if she's someone special, we owe it to her to get her out of it, right?" Devon hadn't stopped moving until he was at the doorway of the second tent. With one last glance at Argoth's glare, Devon stooped to go through the door.

CHAPTER FOUR

MEETING YOUR MATE

In the tent, Eva had closed her eyes and was trying to forget the lovely amber colors she had just seen in another pair. Her life wasn't a pretty one. She didn't deserve any that came to the camp that night, and that included him. Besides, princes were not lovely people - at least, not that she had experienced. They got what they wanted and destroyed it. So, time to stop the fantasy where it had sprung.

She was waiting for the Weylyns to leave. Until then, though, she was in here, in the shared tent alone. The music was delightful, so she let herself dance to it, moving bare feet over mats and furs and blankets.

Devon hadn't wanted to interrupt such a beautiful moment. He would've watched her dance til the sun came up. Alas, he didn't have all night. So, he cleared his throat.

She jumped and twisted, her braid moving with the jostle. Her eyes were wide with surprise, but her hand moved instinctively, ready to fight. Her stance turned her to the side, showing the least amount of body.

"You know how to fight. I'm not sure if I should say I'm impressed or that I'm sorry ya ever had to learn it."

Her eyebrow lifted, and her head tilted slightly. Devon cleared his throat again and bowed to her. His deep voice filled the tent. "Lady, will you do me the honor of a dance?" He would not force her, but hc hoped she'd say yes.

"No one's ever asked me before."

"Then I'm honored ta be the first." He held out his hand.

She looked around and then back at him before nodding. Then she held her hand out to him, waiting to see if he'd take it and how he would.

Stepping forward, Devon took the outstretched hand and held it as if it were porcelain.

She had tight, textured curls that were being forced into a resentful state. The reddish tint to her hair only complimented her coloring and her bright topaz eyes. She was so petite that he looked twice, maybe even three times, her size. But she walked silently at his side all the way to the bonfire.

His grip was not hurtful or controlling, simply proper. When they were at the edge of the dancing bunch, she turned to him and placed a hand on his shoulder, letting him know she would have him lead. Her heart was thumping in her chest. As his hand moved to her waist, his other rested upon her hip. While moving with her, Devon rumbled protectively. Before long, no one else dared come close.

"I'm Devon of Pack Weylyn and you are?" They were already flush against one another and so talking wasn't impossible.

"Evalyn," she whispered, her breathing beginning to move with the flow of his already. He seemed made for her, despite being so much larger. She just fit into that perfect spot with her head on his chest. "Most call me Eva."

"A beautiful name for a beautiful woman." Devon rumbled softly as he drew in her scent. "You're different from the others."

"How so, do ya think?" She was curious to see where this went. She'd been to several cities with Regis' caravan, and there was always a silver-tongued devil amongst those in the crowd. This time, she hoped he wasn't just a charmer. But she expected the words that made her into an object to pop out at any moment.

"In all ways that I can see. Your eyes, the inflections to your voice when you speak, the way you sway your hips just a little with each step. The color of your skin and how it almost hides the scattered freckles over your nose and shoulders. I wonder if your mind is a match to your looks." Devon grinned and his canines were visible as he moved through each step without missing a beat.

"You're asking if my mind is beautiful or strong? I don't follow, sir."

"Both. And though your looks have naught to do with this - I'm hopin' ta find you're smart. Regis says you are trouble, but I see a woman that knows what she wants and just refuses ta take less. So, that's one level of smart right there. You know common, even though yer from the other side. Another. But your looks, they're definitely something I've never seen."

"I began as a human, nearly 30 years ago and as a human, I am of mixed race. That makes me different and unacceptable to most in the world I come from. Then, a lycan turned me. So, my question would be, am I still beautiful to your royal eyes?"

Their steps slowed as he leaned down to rumble against her ear. "Yes, you are. If people where you come from think differently, obviously they're fools across that portal."

"Have you never been?" He legitimately surprised Eva.

"No, why would I? All that I need or could ever want is here in this world." Devon had lifted his brow in curiosity. "Tell me of this other world of yours? Why should it appeal to me?"

"Those like me were born there, and if you like me, then it stands to reason you might very well like the world. So, ya shouldn't be too quick to not want to go." She looked around them. "They've ocean towns there, but with much more greenery. Even the lushest forests here are no comparison. Humans must cut the trees and brush away just to get through to unknown places. And they are learning such marvels. Every year something new has happened." She smiled. "Alas, there's not near the magical energy in the world I come from. And there's but one moon. The one is enough and is powerful. I used to imagine the goddess looking down upon me from the light of the moon and stars."

"You felt the Goddess over there?" This was surprising to hear. "Are you sure there is magic as well? I've been told it left with the Elves and Dragons that fled to our world and others."

"Oh, yes, I believe there are many powers out there that touch our lives. I can feel magic around people, and some have more than others. Certain places have magical energy still all around. And there are still dragons, I believe. They hide like us." Continuing to dance, the couple had their own rhythm on the side of the crowd, lost in one another. "The Goddess, as I speak it - she's found in things, hidden but still there, even in the patriarchal beliefs of these humans. They venerate her but in new ways. Sadly, they uplift their women less than lycan do."

Devon snorted, "Then I was correct. They're indeed fools. Our mates are why we have a life as we do." His head tipped to the side and his beads clicked together. "And what do you do there?"

"I like to help people. All people. I've learned how to heal others, how to fight, how to listen." She shrugged. "How about you, sir?"

"Me? I'm the heir to Pack Weylyn. One day I'll lead it when my father is in the fields. For now, I keep my younger brother and sister out of mess. I scout, keep our enemies at bay, and assure all are safe on our lands." He paused and let their eyes meet again. "You'd like the palace; it's a sight to behold."

"I have seen several palaces here since arriving. I had never laid eyes on one in my world." Eva continued to match every step Devon made. His scent was unique, and his warmth seemed addictive. "My experiences with palaces here have not been good. Not all princes are as kind or proper as you."

"I'm just being myself. Being a prince doesn't bring respect. How you treat others is how you win respect."

Their conversation continued, each exploring more about the other, their world, their lives, and their passions. Eva luxuriated against him whenever she got the chance. At one point, she even placed her head on his chest for a slower few songs.

Several dances later, there was a light tapping on Devon's shoulder.

"Prince? We're waiting."

"Sorry Argoth, I lost track of time." He grinned and flushed a little. "I'll be right there. Just give me a moment."

"You must go?" Eva asked. She wasn't ready.

"Let me take you from this. I can make you so happy if you just give me a chance. I can keep you safe and make you smile. Will you let me do that?"

Derek had been escorting Gareth not far away and both stopped in their tracks when they heard Devon.

"Are you drunk?" Derek asked Devon. "I mean, she's petite, sure, but she's no elf. And a slave? Exactly how'd the prince think such is gonna work out?"

Eva squeezed his hands with her much smaller ones. She looked from the two together back up into his eyes again. He was so noble, and it had nothing to do with his heredity. He truly wanted to save her, didn't he?

"I want to believe that. I want to think your nobility has nothing ta do with your station. But do you know how many times I've heard such words over these last years?" She didn't let go of his hands.

"You've never heard them from me, and I am a lycan of my word. What kind of leader would I be if I broke it?" There was nothing said, but he hadn't let her go.

"You are a royal among a primary pack in this world, Devon of Weylyn. What do you wish to do? Buy me and then make me your courtesan while a mate walks at your side?"

He actually scowled at that idea. "No, I'm not the unfaithful type. I want you for my mate, Eva. I would never dishonor you by making you a courtesan."

"A lovely fantasy." She couldn't hide the tears in her eyes. "May I kiss you, prince? So, I can at least dream of what you're promising me? Or... would you kiss me?"

Slipping his arm around Eva's waist, Dev lifted her to her tiptoes and captured her lips with his own. It wasn't what she expected. There was no rush or roughness. It was slow, enticing, and sensual. He teased her with lips, teeth, and tongue. And he deepened the kiss when she opened to let him.

Oh, she could imagine being made love to by him. She would not wash her clothes for as long as she could manage - she wanted to smell him as long as possible! He tasted wonderful and the way he took her mouth and her... whole being - without a bit of harm? Well, to be honest, she'd never experienced it.

"I'll come back for you, Eva. You have my word on it. I have to find my father to make the arrangements."

Hugging herself as his guard literally tugged and pulled him away, probably to scold him, Eva nodded at his words. She watched them until they were gone. And then she did her best to slip back behind the tents to stay away from anyone else. She didn't want to be touched by anyone. Not after Devon.

"You're worse than these young ones when they catch the scent of a skirt they have an itch for." Argoth chuckled, but that chuckle soon died away when he took heed of Devon. "No." He stopped and watched Devon's eyes glitter and that evil smirk flit over the younger lycan's face. "No! Not her, not *any* slave. Yer ole man is gonna kill us all if you even think it. Not bad enough she's a slave, she's also a turned lycan and from the other world."

"I felt it, Argoth. I felt it inside of me. Just like Mama described it. Everything's right in her arms. She's my mate."

"Are you serious?" Derek laughed wholeheartedly. "So, we get very little to go on from this Regis Caravan Master. We spend coins on nothing. And you come back in a dreamworld - hot for a slave." Derek poked a silent Gareth with his elbow. "Tell him, Gar. Talk some sense into your big brother."

"Good luck brother, you'll need it. Especially if you get your way and make her yours. That one's wild." Gareth patted his brother on the shoulder and pointed at his own eye. "I see a spitfire soul in those eyes. And I should know."

"I wouldn't have her any other way." No one would deter Devon.

"You usually get anything you want, so use that magic you got as the favorite son ta get this. If nothin' else, maybe Pops'll kick yer ass for a while instead of mine." Gareth walked away from Devon and the two guards. Argoth growled and his hand fisted tighter. Derek just rolled his eyes and turned to follow Gareth.

"I didn't mean..."

"He knows that. I know that. You just got that alpha attitude sometimes, Devon. If yer serious about this, maybe Kieran'll give in. You're his heir. Normally, that would make this silliness impossible. A turned lycan slave? Damn. But if you don't back down, who knows?" Argoth put a hand on his friend's shoulder to turn him back toward the trails.

Chapter Five

A REASON TO CONTINUE

"I'M NOT SURE WHAT you want from us. We're not steam machines you can set and forget about. And besides, even those need care and coal." Senias crossed his arms over his chest while standing across the table from Kieran Weylyn.

The alpha has his hair pulled back from his face, and the plaits were not just on one side but made in intricate patterns all the way across his blonde head. He had on the normal cloth pants any person would wear. The dragons also wore such things. But he also had on a silk shirt that hung low to his thighs, gathered at his waist. This was how he looked when he was the ruler of a lycan pack and expected to receive officials from other lands.

They were in his study. The big office held books and tables, which were covered in maps and journals now. Keeping one's people free was a full-time duty, and it wasn't just about the battlefield.

"I want you to live up to yer bargain, Scales. The both of ya signed on ta help us get all the packs free of the slaving. Particularly from the elves of Calen. We're so fuckin' close...I want ta be sure."

"You've had responses from the two outer packs. We even traveled to one other. That's well... not really a pack, but as close to one as you can call it. All those displaced lycan, they've made a home for themselves and they're fine. They haven't seen an elf in the last year thanks to us keeping everything on this side of the Great Gorge. You're waiting for one more. I believe we may be done, Kieran," Inea explained.

"Not til I know for sure. I'm holdin' ya to yer vow." Kieran walked back to the table farther away, the one with the map of the Great Gorge and Ricktor Pass on it. The surrounding lands were all packlands. "I want the trail through the gorge safe for trade again. We've lost so much because of them damned pointy-eared...

"Neither of us is sure of our actions anymore, Kieran. Aren't you hearing us?" Senias followed the Alpha and put his hands on the opposite side of the table from him. He spoke in the lycan's own tongue, showing as much respect as he could by having learned the language of growls and rumbles. "We may soon be as your berserkers, but with no leads."

Kieran grimaced but didn't look up from his studies.

"Imagine us strafing the elves and then not stopping until all that's left on both sides is ash. This world is not treating our minds well. We knew it was a possibility when we first came here." Senias turned slightly to better include Inea in this conversation. "We had no choice. But now, we also have no choice. It's been years. We all know the Crimson organization on the other side... their hunters? They've calmed the hunt. We've been able to find an expert at drafting documents in Iona. This is going to happen, Kieran."

"I need you for just a little longer, Senias." Kieran finally raised his head to face them. "Inea, the elves? They're retreating. Just...stay til we're sure. I don't need ta give 'em an inch." The big alpha stood up when the door swung open suddenly.

"We're back," Gareth called, immediately walking to Inea. His eyes searched hers as he took her hand and stepped closer, letting her put an arm around his shoulder. He rumbled quietly, and the dragoness put her head against his.

The alpha watched but remained where he was; silent. One could tell a lot about a couple when they saw one. He wondered if she'd told his son about her plans to leave. That was a broken heart none of them needed. And how would she continue if Gareth didn't leave with her? Even now, he comforted her - not even realizing what she was upset over. Just his presence and touch had done that. Would he lose his son?

Senias stood back, his eyes following Devon as the elder brother walked into the study a bit more slowly. The male dragon bowed his head slightly out of respect for the elder prince.

"Well, what'd'ya find out?" Kieran asked, before turning to Devon.

"The elves are leaving. They're exiting along the Great Gorge. Regis said he'd witnessed it and got the word from the forest elves of Ricktor Pass. He said Pack Weylyn has nothing to worry about, but that we should be wary about the packs along their path back home."

"Like I said..." Senias pointed out, but he stopped when he heard Kieran's growl.

"You know the Alphas of Rourke were the ones ta take back the lycan slaves from the elves up there and we've not heard from them. Their land butts up against the gorge. These elves are probably looking for some payback. I don't care how refined most of 'em act... they like vengeance as much as the next."

"No doubt. I never said they wouldn't," the dragon replied.

"We need ta defend the other packs and be sure the bastards actually leave. And until we get word from Pack Rourke, I'm gonna assume they may need help. We answer to that, and you answer to us." Kieran and Senias had a tight-lipped standoff happening across the table.

Everyone in the room stood in a silence that seemed to tie their stomachs in knots. Both men were unwavering and then...

"We do this and then we owe you nothing." Senias drew the line.

"Acceptable." Kieran held his arm out over the table. Senias took it, his hand going to the elbow and both grasping the forearm in agreement.

"We make rounds, scouts do their jobs, and you call us in if we're needed for backup?" The dragon waited.

"Sounds like a wise plan. I want to minimize the carnage." Kieran took a deep breath before making his way to his desk. He hadn't expected the next voice he heard. Devon.

"You and I need to talk."

"Well, then talk." Kieran motioned for the chairs across from him. Both dragons looked at one another and then at Devon. Inea was still holding on to Devon's brother like he was her lifeline.

"Alone." He looked towards each one in the room before looking back at Kieran.

"Good to see you, too." Senias chuckled before looking at Kieran for affirmation.

"We can continue tonight. My son needs to talk to me. And it must be damned important." Kieran's steady gaze was on his eldest. Senias walked by

Devon, his eyes looking over his ally as he made his way. Gareth kept his arm around Inea's waist, and they also passed Devon on the way out.

"Good luck," was all the younger brother said. The door closed, and the office became uncomfortably quiet once again.

"Well?"

"Mother needs to send word to Pack Simoa and let them know I will no longer take their daughter as my mate."

Kieran couldn't hold back a chuckle. He could only imagine what kind of reaming he'd get for telling his mate that. She'd been working on this connection to the wily Simoa Pack for years and years.

"I have found my mate and tomorrow I will go to get her." Devon seemed calm, even though his eyes shimmered.

"You went to a slave market caravan worked by Madron Regis. And you found your mate there? She of another pack? Because that might not be so bad—"

"No, she's not of any pack that I know of, and if she is not from this side." Devon took a deep breath and went on, "She is a slave Regis has with his caravan. Her name is Evalyn, she goes by Eva, and I've never found a woman as captivating or enthralling as she is." Devon couldn't help the serene smile that moved over his lips when he spoke of Eva.

Kieran stared blankly at his son. "A slave from the other world?"

"Yes, but she was not always a slave. She is a healer, too - and she's not an elf." Devon grinned, hoping that added bit helped.

"Mmmm…" Kieran nodded at the answer. He stood up and leaned over onto the heavy desk, making it creak. He looked Devon in the eyes. "No."

"Yes." Devon shrugged, "Or I leave my claim as your heir to Gareth and take Eva to live away from the pack."

"For the love of the Goddess, Devon!" Kieran's arms were in the air, his hands clawed but not shifting to stress his words. "Your brother's cock has more sense than that, and he's aimed his sights at a dragoness! At least they're both not only satisfied but the pack gains from the situation! A SLAVE?!?! "

"A healer! And it doesn't matter to me she is a slave right now, as my mate, that will change." Devon never lost his calm way while his father verged on rupturing vessels. "What won't change is my mind. I want her and no other as my mate."

Kieran's big hand moved over his face, and he turned to look out the window.

"She feel the same way? Or she see your standing and know you'd free her and treat her good, so she's willing to take yer hand?" he looked over his shoulder at Devon.

"Yes, she feels the same way." Devon held his father's hard gaze. "I'd hope that she knows I'll treat her good, but of course, she isn't in it for my position."

"How do you know?" The Alpha turned to study his son. He wasn't thinking clearly. He needed to think clearly. Kieran was torn. He didn't want his sons to be forced into something, and he didn't want them taken advantage of. He knew how that played out.

"Because my gut tells me so and so did her eyes. Eva didn't ask this of me. She was happy enough with our dancing. I told her I wanted her as my mate. She tried to talk me out of it, just as you are. I'm not easily dissuaded. Guess she'll find that out. She seemed convinced I wouldn't return."

There was a knock on the door and Argoth opened it to stick his head in. "Pardon the interruption, but we're needed in the western borders. There's some trouble stirrin' that the scouts say needs our attention, Dev."

The low growl that emanated from Kieran was the sort that didn't carry far. He just watched the messenger for a moment.

"I'll be out soon, Argoth. Get the others ready." Devon watched the door close again before returning his gaze to his father. "I'm serious about this, but if you want to find out for yourself, go see her. Don't make trouble though, because even if I have to track her to the other world, I will."

"Your focus should be on protecting the packlands - all of them. Get the elves out, don't fuck 'em. We're almost at a point where those bastards are no trouble. We need to finish this so your pups can live in peace someday." Kieran placed his hand on the desk and said nothing more about the subject at hand.

"You want my mind on protecting the packlands? Give me a reason to protect them. Get me my mate." Devon stepped closer and pushed his hand down to slam on the desktop, forcing his father to look into his eyes. "I felt it in my soul, papa. Just like Mama told me it felt. I never thought I'd feel it, not after going through so much, after all these years. But I felt it to my soul."

Kieran's hard stare changed when he heard Devon describe what he had felt. "Your Mama told you?"

"Yeah, and it was real. I never believed it before. But I felt it." Devon swallowed. His voice wasn't much more than a whisper. "Papa, I'm tired of war. I saw my brothers die. I've been stuck in a mine for prisoners. The elves just don't seem to want ta go from our lands. Either give me a reason..."

"I'll consider it. I'll go see her. That's all I can promise."

Devon nodded. "It's enough. You'll know when you meet her. I'm sure."

"But what's important right now? Is protecting the packlands and giving those Weylyn fighters a leader to follow. The dragons have a plan. If you need ta defend Pack Rourke lands and split off others to go where the dragons go, then so be it. I'll join up as soon as I can get there. And then you and your brother come home to ya mama. I don't want her heart hurt anymore."

"Yes sir, we'll handle things and be home before Mama even misses us." He gave a quick bow to his Alpha out of respect before turning to take his leave.

Kieran crossed his arms over his chest and watched Devon's back as he exited the study.

"Don't make him be like us, Kieran," the feminine voice came from the back of the room. There were secret passages all in this place, and one led from his office to the private chambers upstairs. He would recognize the voice anywhere.

"You mean, like you?" The big Alpha turned to look at his mate. She was breathtaking. And the painful expression she gave him just caused him more heartache. "Apologies, Helena." His shoulders drooped a little.

"I suppose I deserved it." She walked forward. Her small hand moved to his enormous arms. "You're a good man, Kieran... under all that gruff. I know that. I've seen it. That's why you'll make the right decision."

He placed a hand over hers and looked into her eyes. He wanted to feel the stirring in his soul; What his son described? But then Helena simply gave Kieran a melancholy smile before pulling her hand back and turning to walk away. He'd never felt that sensation Devon had talked about. She had...but not with him. Who was he to take it away from his son?

CHAPTER SIX

WHEN WAR IS TOO FAMILIAR

THE LANDS ON THE side of the Great Gorge traditionally belonged to Pack Rourke. Devon's men were moving to the perimeter, but local scouts that had gone before them came to Devon to report.

"I haven't seen the Rourke perimeter patrol. I had friends among them. It's not like them to not hang about, even after they're done. I haven't heard the guards. This morning, I saw one horse out in the woods where I had camped. They take better care of their animals than that."

Devon scowled as he looked towards the Pack lands in question. Madron Regis had alluded to the possibility that Weylyn blood wasn't what the elves had come for. Scouts had seen elves packing their equipment and leaving earlier in the week - not long after their last battle.

~ Devon, we've made our flyovers of the gorge. Perhaps the elves have gotten the idea to move on? Would you like us to go on to the castle of Pack Rourke? ~

They were words spoken by Senias but in his mind. Devon grimaced, for mind speak wasn't his favored method of communication. Unlike his brother and father, he was unaccustomed to mental intrusions. He remembered speaking like this to Senias on maybe two occasions. So, this was halting, but convenient. He slowed his pace and concentrated on the dragon and the words.

~ Yes. Tell us anything we should know. ~

"You okay?" Argoth asked.

"Yeah, Sen was just asking if they should go on to the castle." Devon began jogging that way again.

"Don't let yer ole man know his dragon's talkin' to you on the regular now. He might get jealous."

"You don't know the half of it." Devon noted the curious expression on Argoth's face, but he opted to shift, not talk. In his full dire wolf form, a huge shaggy blond-white creature with shimmering amber eyes, he had the excuse of not being able to talk. He didn't want to consider that his father might very well deny him his mate...and then what he and Gar had walked in on at the castle.

Things were changing, and Devon did not know if they were changing for the good anymore. The rest of the lycan followed their leader's example and trotted along in small groups dotted along the perimeter and closed inward.

First, there was a long, mournful howl, letting them all know something was wrong. Devon was about to take off running, but he looked above him to see the nearly black dragon, maroon scales of his underbelly reflecting the sun's light. The gigantic creature moved over them, and Devon had to shake himself out of the awe he felt. The sound and feel of displaced air weren't as bad as he expected. But why was the dragon moving so fast?

The wolves shivered and whined as a scream-like roar pierced the sounds of the forest!

The scraping of metal on metal was the closest thing Devon could imagine. It was not like anything he had heard! Devon shook his head, his ears aching from the sound. He watched as a black-furred wolf bolted from the rest. Gareth...had it been Inea? Devon put his muzzle in the air and howled for his groups to be wary, but to move forward. Argoth took off after Gareth.

~ It's poisoned! ~ Inea had run back from the fields where she had landed and was wiping her claws on the ground nearby to get it off. Senias landed near her and then moved toward her before sitting on his hind legs to look over her clawed palms. The two dragons were taller than most of the scrub trees in the area. Blisters formed on the pads of her clawed hands where the scales didn't cover. There was a mournful, painful sound coming from her chest, and it wasn't just about the physical pain. ~ Are there any left? All I saw... they were dead... ~

~ Did we check on the elves, too late, Devon? ~ Senias asked, knowing the lycan would soon come forward. ~ Be careful what you touch. The fields are covered in lye and scattered with salt and…the dead. There's no smell. They aren't rotting, but I think they're dead. ~ Senias warned.

Devon howled the orders for his lycan to stop and not cross into the primary fields of settlement. He shifted and made sure his boots were intact before walking further. Devon made his way forward cautiously.

Gareth shifted back into his human form next to Inea. "There's a creek just down these trails. I'll show ya the way, Nea. Let's get you washed up!"

Inea shifted in a flash of light to her human form. She was holding her hands palm up, and the blisters were still there. The young lycan literally lifted his lady from the ground to carry her to the water.

Devon and his brethren had made their way through the trails leading to the main gates of Pack Rourke land. There were no guards. All the vegetation looked wilted. Littered all over the fields were dead people. He felt a chill race up his back.

He and Argoth looked to either side of the main cobblestone road and saw nothing but bodies. They had warily stepped through the fields to check for pulses, but there was nothing. They were all dead, but not decomposing. Whatever the elves had used bought them the time they needed to wipe out this pack and then prepare for a long journey back to their homeland.

The enormous black dragon flew over them to the central courtyard. He was sniffing the air. Battlements and homes were all devastated. The main palace area of this castle complex - half of it was simply…gone.

The castle felt hollow as they all searched it for survivors. Such a loss of life was heartbreaking. Devon came back out from the throne room and down the stairs, past what had been beautiful gardens and fresco paintings.

"They wiped the Pack out. The Alpha and his mate are dead, along with their unborn. I can't find their son… he's not among the dead that I see. Come to think of it, I've only seen one dead pup. This didn't just happen, Sen. So, yes, my friend. It seems we were too late." Devon couldn't help but wonder - what might've happened had they not taken longer? Had they not stopped to rest? Had they not gone to the slaver's camp? Could they have stopped this?

Devon set his people to get the shaman. They needed a safe method of gathering the dead.

"There's a lack of children," Derek pointed out to the others. His father was quick to answer.

"The last lycan slaves. They took the pups ta spit in our faces." The lycan scout growled with an unexpected viciousness. "We can't just let them have those pups."

"I know," Devon muttered. So much for wishing that this would all be over. He turned when he heard horses. He howled a warning but was relieved to get a howl back. It was his father.

Kieran came from the west with ten of his own personal guards. Once he had stopped in front of Devon, the Alpha put his hand back behind him. A small tawny-skinned woman with a large plait of reddish hair hopped down with the swing of his big arm. She had a bag with her and rushed to the obviously injured woman that stood taller than the dark-haired lycan she was in front of.

"What's happened?" Eva asked.

The sight of Eva surprised Devon and elated him at the same moment. His joyful greeting for her would have to wait, though.

"I only stepped into the mix with my front claws. That's all it took," she explained to the woman. "I'm a dragon. Our wounds sometimes get better if we shift forms, but it didn't completely heal. And I need to move some bodies..."

"Here, I have some salve that'll help with it. If ya don't mind," Eva dug in her bag, produced a jar, and opened the lid. The smell was nice, lemony and when she spread it gently on Inea's hands, the sorceress took a deep breath and smiled at the woman.

"It cools. I...expected the opposite." Inea let her gaze move to her dragon partner, who was worried over her. Then to Gareth. "I'll be fine, I think. She helped."

"It's a mixture of some things I brought from the other world and some herbs I found here. Should heal you up quicker and maybe give relief?"

"It does." Inea smiled. "Who are you?"

"You're a healer?" It mystified Gareth.

"Yes. It's my specialty. Along with some other things." She looked around. "Anyone else need help?"

"She's the one my brother wants," Gareth whispered to Inea.

"Have you found the Alphas? Their son?" Kieran asked all around.

"Alphas are dead, no sign of their son. Might be with survivors somewhere tucked away." Devon needed to help this Pack all that he could. He had a duty. And now, he also needed to find justice for Pack Rourke... as they had been allies. He also needed to find the children. They could no longer just threaten to take out the elves. Not when those elves had pups as prisoners. "The dead are bein' gathered for a pyre to send 'em to the fields together. Sen and now Nea should be able to help gather using their claws."

Eva swallowed, shocked at seeing so much death. "How is it they aren't... they don't stink of death, you know?" she asked.

"It's a spell. Eternal Sleep. They're dead. But they don't rot. We'll have to break it and burn them to send them off," Inea explained.

"It'd be a curse on this land, is what they've tried to do." Eva spoke in her old tongue and made a symbol of sorts with her fingers. "May the lady revisit upon the elves threefold as they've done to her people." She moved off toward where she saw the others pushing debris around. They were all searching in a kitchen area. She could make out what was left of a huge oven. "There is some green energy within this place. There is life here, yet."

"You have the sight?" Senias asked the woman.

"If that be what you call it. I see energies." Eva pointed to where the energy was brightest.

Wasting no time, Devon went to help clear the way into the area she spoke of. The others rushed with him to clear out rubble by making a chain. He looked up at the lycan behind him and realized it was his father. Devon felt a tightness in his chest but fought it. His father was right behind him, for the ole Alpha had been good friends with the peaceful agrarians who were Pack Rourke. This pack had given them a good place of fortification against the Elves of the Northern Kingdoms for years. Apparently, they could not keep themselves safe in the exodus.

"Eva, did you still see it?" Devon asked.

"I...no, Devon, it was so weak. I know it was in that area, where you are." She moved over to where everyone was trying to dig their way through the rubble. Then she sucked in a breath. "Yes! I still see it. It's so faint."

Senias moved past. "Maybe I can finish this up?" he offered. He moved along the back of the wall. "There is a space beneath. A hidden cubby! We need to get what's left of this wall out."

Eva waited while the others continued to clear the debris. She would be ready to treat whoever came out. She noticed the sorceress was also helping, using a stone hung around her neck. Their eyes met. They were both trying to help ease pain. She had found someone that she had that in common with. Eva felt better.

Crouching down where the dragon had motioned, Devon peered in and huffed, "Can't reach, but Gareth can."

When his brother called his name, Gareth moved into the room and crouched down to look in. "Why the hell did the pup get crammed into such a place?" He shivered but laid himself out on his belly and moved into the cubby.

"When ya get in there, cover yourselves up so we can bring the rest of the wall down." Dev rumbled as Gareth vanished from sight.

"Yeah, yeah, just hurry the fuck up. I may be little, but that don't mean I like tight spots." Gareth growled as he made his way in to find whoever was there. After just a few beats, they could hear Gareth yelling, "Got him! It's a kid!"

Looking at Sen, Devon rumbled, "Okay, let's get 'em out of there now."

"Move back out of this place," Senias ordered. They all knew to obey the dragon when he said something like that. The human form of the dragon moved his hands into the opening of the small tunnel Gareth had just gone into. In a flash of light, he let his magic morph him back into his dragon form, and the entire place rumbled. Stones and glass fell off his enormous back, but his claws wound up perfectly surrounding the place where Gareth had gone.

"Eva, Inea, come look at him and see what can be done," Devon called to their healers. The dragon gently placed Gareth and the young boy he was carrying on the ground. Devon inspected the boy. "It's Rory...the son of the Alphas. A prince of Pack Rourke."

Both women hurried, Inea moving her injured hand up and around the kid's face. Her magical energy moved outward, coaxing him away from the fields and back to the world of the living. Eva went right to work on getting a water skin and trying to get the boy to drink.

"He's horribly dehydrated. His nails and hands are a mess. He must've gotten stuck in there," Inea whispered.

"Can you help me make him swallow?" Eva asked the dragoness.

"Yes," the woman placed her hands appropriately beneath Rory's neck and head, despite her pain. As Eva slowly let some water go into his mouth and down his throat, Inea would move him so that the water would go properly and not down into his lungs. She only did this maybe four times before there were signs of stirring.

There was a cough and wheeze as Rory sucked in the air. A few long seconds passed before he did the same and he repeated the action three more times over the next three minutes. His eyes barely opened, as if he just didn't have the strength for more than the barest response.

"Let's get him outta here," Kieran called to the others. "Senias, cast a portal. Argoth, take the pup to the shaman. Everybody needs to return to the castle proper. Lady Helena can sort things out from there. We need ta discuss the next plan of action."

The two dragons let their gazes touch. There was a nod. Acceptance. Devon recognized it for what it was. Things had changed. Therefore, the plans for departure had changed.

"We'll give the rest the proper send-off if Inea can figure out how to end this Eternal Sleep curse." Kieran slipped back into the role of Alpha and the lycan in charge. Devon let him. He wasn't sure if that made him a coward or what, but he just needed to move away. He turned and came face to face with Eva.

"Didn't expect my ole man to be the one to get ya. I planned on doin' it myself. I just needed other things ta change and his permission." He looked around at all that was going on. "Not exactly the welcome I was plannin' for ya." Knowing his palms were filthy, Devon lifted his hand to brush his knuckles over her cheek instead.

"I could've stayed back at the palace, but my heart wanted to come to you. And it's a good thing. I help people. I heal people. Therefore, it was all good timing, by the Goddess."

"I'm glad you came." Devon smiled despite the hideous world around him. He had a reason to keep fighting now... and it wasn't just for freedom or justice. Eva was his future, and he wanted to be sure that war wasn't looming over their shoulders. He had a reason to finish this.

CHAPTER SEVEN

THE WAY HOME

THE FILTHY PAIR WERE strolling back from Pack Rourke's lands through the forest and onto the paths that led back to Pack Weylyn. Their scouts and dragons were monitoring where the elves got to. There was nothing to be done right then but help Rory and clean up the other pack. They had been doing so for hours and all of them were exhausted. Devon hoped the elves didn't force them to make moves too soon.

"I'll take my answer now."

"Answer?" Eva turned her gaze to Devon.

"Will ya be my mate?" Devon asked after wiping his hands off his pants. He needed a break, as did everyone else here. And for his father to have brought the woman he knew in his soul to be his mate - here? There was no truer test of her grit and her strength. He held his hand out to her, and she accepted the gesture, her smaller fingers entwined with his. He tugged her closer as they walked toward the road that would eventually lead them to his home.

"But... mate? Is it a vow or is it magical bonding or...I... I don't know your culture well, Devon. I want to be with you and get to know you. It would be nice to learn more about you and your people. And I want you to do the same with me - at least the *knowing me* part. Would they accept me as your mate? Some cultures they have very strict rules for these things."

"Do they, now?" Devon smirked, his eyes smiling as he looked her way.

"There are things that come with me. I'm not innocent like some males would want. I've had children in the other world and dealt with pain. We've not told each other about ourselves. I came here to help everyone. And now, that means you. So, before I answer, let's go back to wherever is your home, and let's learn about each other."

Instead of being upset, which she probably expected, Devon's smile brightened. "We can court first so we get to know each other, but it won't change my mind. Six moons is usual courtin' time with our Pack unless ya want longer. I'm willing to wait. My mind and soul have already decided. They decided the night we danced."

"I don't know that I need six moons, Devon." As they walked, she shivered.

"Fair enough. When yer ready, we'll be more."

"How are you so sure of yourself and of this?"

Devon just grinned. "Tell me somethin' about yerself."

She swallowed and nodded, looking straight ahead.

"Most important thing - I do not abide liars. And I do not abide disloyalty. I do not want more than you, and you should not want more than me. If we are to be mates, those two things you must agree upon first."

"I don't lie and don't abide liars myself. We're of the same mind there. I don't need or want more than you, Eva. My desire is only for one. I will not stray or play ya false." Devon shook his head slowly as they walked. "It isn't in me to do so."

"Now then, I will not abide abuse. Either way. I've felt it. I never want to feel it again. That is not what love is. But some? They don't understand this. Do you?"

"The only ones that feel my fists are my enemies." Devon paused in their walk and waited for her to turn. He slowly lifted his free hand to cup her cheek. The move wasn't quick nor rough, it was slow and gentle for one his size. "I would never hurt ya Evalyn. I want to protect ya and as my mate, I'll make sure none ever harm ya again. They'll have to go through me first and I won't make it easy."

Devon knelt before the beauty that had him so enthralled. "I don't know what all you've been through, but I will tell you this." His accent was gone as he became serious. "I'm a lycan and son to the Alpha. One day I will be the leader he is, so I will need a strong mate to be Alpha at my side. Most lycan are loyal and take one mate. We don't treat our mates badly because it is wrong and dishonorable. Our mates are our lives, Eva." He brought her hand to his face and rubbed her palm over his cheek as he rumbled for her from deep in his chest. "You bring life into the world, help us thrive, love us, care for us, raise our young with us, and help us teach them. Our mates hold more power over us than most understand."

Eva didn't take her eyes off him.

"As our heart and soul, our mates can calm us even at our worst rages." Drawing Eva closer, Devon moved her hand down to his broad chest and laid it over his pounding heart. "You can also unleash our inner beast faster than even we can draw that out. We wilt and fade without our mates. We become lost. I'm telling you this so that you understand abuse from me in any form will not happen. Ever."

Eva tilted her head slightly and her eyes moved to where he had placed her hand. She had already been using her gifts all day. He figured she was doing more now. There were probably things she had yet to tell him. Devon hoped she understood nothing would make him want her less. She stayed quiet, listening, watching, and letting herself feel him, so he went on.

"You say that you've had pups as if that would deter me. I don't care. If your pups still live, we will get them. They become mine when you are mine and I am yours. No questions, Eva. And as for the Pack, they will love you. If they don't, I will handle it. But from what I've seen you do already, you are gaining respect among them." He was still kneeling and smiled at her as he lifted her hand from his chest to kiss her knuckles.

She pulled her hand from his grasp, and she placed her lips upon his. Her arms went around his neck. Eva did not let go of him for a while. She heard footsteps, but neither of them gave a damn. Once the kiss was done, they were both catching their breath.

"Your father bought me from the slavers. He had told me how this would work, and said if I wanted to stay, he would be sure they accepted me. He told me, if I wanted to go, I was free. I'm free either way and if I stay, I get to be mates with the one person I've always dreamt about. So..." She smiled and pressed her forehead to his, "I told you we probably wouldn't need six months."

Her taste was still on his lips. Devon rumbled even deeper for her as his arms went around Eva's waist to keep her nice and close. "Good, because I don't want to wait that long to make you my mate."

"I want to learn how to be who I am."

"I think between me and my mama, we can help you with that. My sister, Alexis? She'll love havin' you. If the elves are truly gone, we have a few days before the next full moon and that gives you time to prepare. My mama will be more than happy to help you, as will I." Devon couldn't resist at least nuzzling his nose along Eva's jaw to her ear, rumbling in his delight and happiness.

Her own smaller rumbling sound answered his and she then almost hiccupped from surprise.

"Why'd you stop yerself?"

"Wasn't sure it was what I should do." She felt the heat on her cheeks, and she averted her eyes out of habit.

"It's our wolves speaking, Eva. That's who we are. It was perfect. You'll learn." Devon placed his fingers beneath her chin to lift her gaze to his. "Never think you must do that with me. Don't be ashamed of who ya are and never act like yer secondary. You're the most important soul in the world to me and we're equals. Got it?" He kept them that way until she nodded the affirmative.

"I can't wait to learn. No one ever taught me. Not the right things. Not about what's inside me. I feel so much more when we're touching, like this - like at the dance." She sighed as she took a seat on his knee and let him hold her. Eva exhaled and allowed herself to relax.

One hand moved around her back for support. Devon took in her scent and rumbled more, deeper from his chest. His other hand took hers. "My mate."

"Is it bad that we feel so happy while all of this sadness is around us?" she whispered in his ear. Right now, it looked as though the warrior was getting helped by his mate through a rough time. And maybe that was partially true.

"Any that have survived, they know their loved ones have gone to the fields, so they would not frown upon our happiness. Matings and births are blessed occasions with lycan. Their hearts ache, but they will still be happy for us. It's how our people are. Grief is heavy and sometimes, if it is too heavy, pack try to help one another through. We'll be here for the survivors, and we'll help them as we can. But we've both been through so much, Eva. I think they can allow us some respite?" Again, his words showed the education his position afforded him. He wasn't ashamed of that. Devon drew her to him as he stood up, her feet barely touching the ground when he did.

Just with that movement, her immediate response was to rumble and then whine, her body stretching languidly on him before relaxing again. She shook her head, rubbed her face against him, and giggled.

Devon held Eva, and his head tipped back to howl. He let the Pack know Eva had accepted and would be his mate. There were howls in return from all over and those walking around them congratulated them with the lycan growls and rumbles they were due. When Devon looked down at her again, it was with a smile.

"I'll teach ya the old tongue if ya want to learn it. We speak it here a lot cause of the elders."

"Please? And sorry about the noise. It's as if I can't help it..." She settled back on the ground but stayed close to him.

"First lesson I can teach about bein' lycan is that it's easy bein' lycan." He chuckled, "Don't fight yer wolf, accept her, and she'll become second nature to ya."

"Oh? So... so it's accepted? I don't have to always worry with courtly manners and constantly control what I feel about the urges to do?"

"Naaaa, we're all similar here. Everybody does things and makes sounds that're instinctual. No need ta be ashamed or hide it."

"I mean, I have common sense. I wouldn't do anything bad or rude, but - I'm not sure where the line is on the other stuff. When I was with the vampire coven, they didn't allow us to growl or make a lot of noise that was - *distasteful*. And shifting wasn't allowed unless we were to fight. As a slave, there were rules..."

"Yer not a slave anymore, Eva. Yer a free woman." Devon seemed stern about those words when he spoke them. "Even if we're mates, you have yer own mind and heart. Yer gonna find it's a lot different with us. Though my mama can be a bit on the prim-n-proper side, so don't let that scare ya off." They turned to continue following the others. Devon kept her close, and his arm stayed around her. "Noises are welcome, as is enjoying life. Now then, tell me what ya do know about being lycan."

Eva looked down. "Devon, I know little more than violence surrounding it. And pain. Normal lycan lives - that was something the vampires didn't allow..."

"Being a lycan isn't a curse, as it seems they taught you. Our customs and culture make our people wondrous, as does the fact that with our shifting' we are closer to nature than even elves can be." He smiled warmly at her and when she let him get close again, he rubbed his nose against hers. Like most lycan, he was very affectionate with his mate, but then, Devon was warm-natured anyway. The prince just didn't get to show it much. He wanted to help heal the wounded soul of the beautiful woman in front of him. He hoped she was going to help heal him from all the heartache he had built up over the years of war. "Thank you for giving me the chance."

CHAPTER EIGHT

DRAGONS & PAIN

SENIAS WOKE WITH A start, jumping from the bed. He left his room and threw open the main door. The draconic man stopped only when he was looking out over the rolling hillside beyond the cabin he occupied. With a shove to the railing, he moved on down the stairs and began running. His bare feet ignored the pinecones, briars, and stones. His heart was pumping like he was being chased by some horrible monster.

But... wasn't he the monster?

At the edge of the stream, he slid in the mud to a stop, and rested his hands on his knees, his breath coming in heaving bursts. His eyes focused on the water, and he moved forward, onto his hands and knees. The man was through the mud and into the shallow water in a side catch, where the water was placid. He looked into his reflection. His cheeks sunken, bags beneath his eyes, Sen's chest, and upper body...so much smaller than he ever remembered. Had he even had any food since coming back?

His gaze remained focused on the water, his vision becoming hazy as he thought back over his last life. He felt hands move over his shoulders to rest on his chest. There in the water's reflection, he could see lively brown eyes set in a porcelain face over his shoulder. There was soft pink around the edges of those eyes. Raven hair clashed with his own wild locks of auburn. His filthy hands moved up his body to touch the hands on his chest.

"Wake up, Senias. You faded again." Inea's soft voice broke his reverie. Blinking violently, the man on his knees realized the reflections in the water were real, but one was his mate and not his kindred. Her blonde hair fell in waves down her shoulder and chest, her green eyes concerned for him. He squeezed her hands and let his head bow.

"I miss him. I never realized how it would feel to not...*feel* him." A tear fell from his eyes. "I need to gather myself." He let her go and turned to raise himself up from the ground. All those pains he had ignored now hit his mind, and he grimaced.

"I understand, Sen. I've not slept a full night in months. We're both experiencing these things, love." Inea walked closer to the stream, wetting her skirts in one place, and then she came back to him and took his hand, and wiped it with the edge. "I know the boy hit us both hard, too. So, we want the ones that comfort us most to be here, holding our hearts."

"He was older. But still just a child. They didn't care. There were children..." Senias took a deep breath. "I pray to whatever thing listens to the prayers of the hopeless every night that my breath has never touched a child. I could never forgive myself."

"I know," Inea whispered, her smile sad as she finished with his hands. "What are we to do? Do you think the elves are done? I know Kieran and many others want revenge. Justice for Pack Rourke. I can't blame them."

"Then they'll need to seek it without us. I don't believe we can risk it anymore. Do you? These dreams? The waking nightmares? The horrible feelings that I catch in my heart? Sometimes, I'm not sure what's real and what's not. Just like when you came upon me. What if my dream had been about something worse? What might I have done?" He shook his head. "No. I won't risk my worst nightmare against people who have helped us and trust us."

"I...I don't know what to do."

Senias paused and looked the woman over. She dressed like a lycan woman, in her skirts and sleeveless wrapping at her breasts. It was telling. The male dragon stepped closer to her and picked up the beautiful pale blue bead she wore around her neck on a thin silver chain.

"Do you..."

"Yes. I know what it means. You think I'm stupid?" she snapped.

Senias took a step back and just looked at her. Her hands were balled into fists and then released over and over. Her frown was deep and Inea brought her arms over herself as if she could protect something she'd already handed over.

"I can't stay and I'm trying to convince him to go," she whispered, wiping her eyes.

"You've told him, then?"

"Not in so many words. I'm trying to ease him into it. He's just...he's not even curious about our world. I had thought there would be a minor curiosity. The truth is, he only wants to know about my life and how dragons live in general. He thinks it'd be easier for us to stay here. But he doesn't seem to want to know about Seamus or his family. I confuse him sometimes, but I just don't think he can imagine it."

"He's in love with you, Inea. And Gareth is so young compared to anyone else. I can't believe you bedded him and not Derek. At least Derek's practical and he's curious about everything! He probably would've been more than happy to go with us to the other side of the portals. Problem solved."

"But that's not reality, Sen. Gareth is my lover, and I ... I love him, too." She bit her bottom lip and turned away from the shocked expression on her mate's face. "Go on... get your jabs in. I know you want to."

Senias suddenly felt very ashamed. He swallowed, and his gaze faltered. He turned back to the stream to look once again at the sparkling surface. The moon had shifted, and the water no longer allowed him a mirror. The dragon supposed that was a good thing.

"I contacted the processor in Iona. Our credentials should be ready within a week. Therefore, we need to figure all of this out before then." He felt her closeness. Her shoulder was against his. Senias slowly turned his head so she could see his eyes. "I would never make fun of your carefree ability to just leap into love. I wish I had been as willing in the past. I'm jealous."

Inea took his arm, and he welcomed her to lean her head on his shoulder.

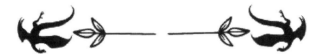

ON THE HILLSIDE OVERLOOKING the two dragons, a large gray wolf sat. His black and white markings made his fur look like it was glowing in the moonlight. His ear twitched, and he got up to follow them a few paces, but then he thought better of it. He huffed before turning to take off in a run—away from the cabins. He was alone on the night that he should have been loved by his mate.

The world was a mysterious thing. The huge Alpha stopped at a stone fence and then moved beyond it to walk among stones placed beneath a great oak tree. His nose huffed against two in particular. There was a soft whine from deep in his chest before the wolf began running again.

He ran through the streams further in the mountains to the northeast. The forest folded in around him and soon he was coming to the land where the night sky filled with sparkling, flying embers. Flames held up their fiery arms, releasing the souls of the dead. Lycan spirits went to the golden fields where their family and friends who were still there waited to run with them. The Alpha remained out of sight, listening to their sorrow. He listened to their plan to get the missing back to their pack. He knew that without help, they would fail and end up in the fields. Kieran walked past and took off running again.

He found himself retracing the march that the elves must have taken from the Rourke Packlands. There was very little scent to go off. That was odd, but it didn't matter. He knew where they were heading and what passages they had to go through to get to their home.

He was going to prove to them that this needed to happen. There were missing pups and lycan still out there. The elves had left the Rourke packlands barren and killed his friends. He had nothing to celebrate. His son finding his mate? Maybe. But should he? Was he allowed? Looking up, Kieran stopped. He'd lost the scent. He could see lights in the valley below.

The dire wolf found his way to the next pack over. The village was now resettled and repaired since Pack Weylyn had saved them the year before, Kieran padded closer and closer to the back of the inn. He made a very high-pitched sound that came from the back of his throat and vibrated his vocal cords. Then, he waited.

A lovely woman snuck quietly from the back door of the kitchen. She looked around to be sure no one saw her before she made her own responding whine. Kieran's ears flinched, and he responded in kind again. She smiled and went scampering off through the dew-damp grass to the edge of the woods and came upon Kieran as he shifted to his human form.

"Alpha Weylyn...I'd thought you moved on," she whispered. Her eyes searched his as he moved closer. Kieran said nothing before bending down to kiss her passionately. She whimpered but didn't pull away. When he released her lips, he slipped a leather necklace over her hair, a wooden carving of a wolf's howling head on it.

She moved her fingers over the intricately carved details, and she smiled before looking up into his amber eyes. Then, she was hopping up to put her arms around his neck and she kissed him again. Her fingers went into the unbraided dark gold mane. Kieran needed no urging. He turned her, flipped up her skirt, and soon buried himself in her. He needed to lose himself to lust.

CHAPTER NINE

MEETING THE MOTHER

FOR THE FIRST TIME in a very long time, Devon had slept in. Which left his mother to introduce Eva to her new world. Helena was in the main hall looking over the plans for the day when she caught sight of the redhead.

"Good morning, Lady Eva, I trust you slept well? Sit and join me for breakfast. Devon will be down shortly and if he isn't, we'll go see what ails him." Helena motioned towards the chair beside her and smiled.

Eva bit one of her thumbnails as she made her way to the woman. She was wearing the clothing that she found in the chair in her room. It fit decently, but Helena could tell that the more petite woman had tied a few things here and there and had rolled the waist of her skirt.

"Devon says you have a beautiful soul, and I believe you are quickly laying claim to his heart."

"He's captured my heart, too, ma'am." Eva looked around the tables and then at the doorway that led to the kitchen.

"He says that you need some guidance in our ways. I'm happy to help." Helena looked the younger woman over. "First things first, we need to get you some clothing. Per my son's request, you are to have a complete wardrobe."

"I only had what I wore. I soiled it while helping with the injured. So, I'm thankful that you lent me these. I'd hate to run around the place naked." She smirked, a gleam in her eyes.

"Oh, well, we wouldn't want that." The lovely brown-haired woman raised a brow.

"Sorry, was that inappropriate humor? I was raised around a lot of men and my mother was not exactly traditional. In the coven, I was mostly around men and other women who were young, so I realized a few years back I might've picked up a crude tongue. Sometimes when I'm nervous, I forget to filter myself."

"Inappropriate humor we can deal with. Just make sure it's not used out when around others of a higher station or representatives of other groups of people. As Devon's mate, you will one day be Alpha to this Pack along with him. You want people to respect you and so you must learn to be a lady that is due that respect." Helena saw great promise in Evalyn. She was just a little rough around the edges. "Now tell me what style of clothing you prefer?"

"I love skirts and light shirts. Sometimes, I've taken the sleeves off regular ladies' blouses. I don't like the fashion of wearing corsets back home. Those things hurt and don't help me much at all. And I like nothing frilly because frilly impedes being practical. Frilly is for special occasions - that and lacey. Just my opinion." She took a deep breath after spilling everything so quickly.

There was a soft laugh from the Alpha as she waved her hand and had food brought out to the table. After all, Eva had been looking toward where the delicious smells were coming from.

"Eat and we will have the seamstress take your measurements, after. That way, your clothing will fit appropriately with a full tummy. I am sure we can come up with suitable and acceptable clothing for you. They will have at least two sets ready by this afternoon." As they filled their plates, Helena continued, "We will also have your attire made for your ceremony. Have you any thoughts on the design?"

"I don't know, what is the ceremony like?" Eva asked quietly before crunching into some crispy bacon. She had her plate full and even went back for the well-seasoned potatoes.

"You can get up and get more when you're done with the first plate, you know?" Helena commented.

Eva nodded, a bit of red moving over the tops of her cheeks when she took her seat. But the bacon didn't make it back to her seat. It was gone.

"Never been to a full moon ceremony?" That was surprising to hear, but the lady shrugged and took a bite of eggs to enjoy before she went on. "We will soon remedy that. Our ceremonies aren't overly grand, not since the wars. The lady dresses as she desires. We mark her with the lycan markings for protection, happiness, fruitfulness, strength, devotion, wisdom, and love."

"Does that work? Or is it like the prayers given back on the other world, where they are a reminder of what we expect between two people and the communities they join?" Eva scooped up some eggs with the potatoes and put them into her mouth. She did not suppress a groan of appreciation, and her eyes glanced over to Helena, obviously worried about what the matron would say.

"For many, they work. The Goddess chooses whom she blesses. You're a healer, so perhaps she will indeed fully bless you." Helena decided not to comment on the girl's table manners. After all, their cooks were extremely talented, and Eva had probably not enjoyed such comforts in a while.

Eva nodded. Her face was too full of food to actually speak. So, Helena moved on.

"At any rate, someone will also paint the male of the set with similar symbols. For it is not only one person's responsibility to keep the couple together and thriving." Helena took a drink before continuing. "This ceremony will be larger than any we've had in some time. All our warriors are home. So, his father, Kieran, will join you before all the Pack and several visiting Packs. You will dance and feast and then Devon will take you away for several days so that you may properly bond without interruptions."

"I kind of can't wait for the taking away and bonding part," the impish grin was unmistakable. "But I am very thankful he's patient. I told him that because of how they treated me after... the change... I didn't know much about my wolf. And he's going to teach me. I feel like, until I met him, I was missing a piece of myself... and not just because I didn't have him in my life. It's more because I wouldn't allow part of me to be... me." She nodded, pleased with how she had explained it.

"When you come back, we will start your lessons and you will learn to be a lycan of our kind and also an Alpha." Helena had watched the young woman's reactions. The matriarch smiled to see that Eva was taking it all in good measure.

"I also can't wait to learn more about being an Alpha. I hope I'm suited for it. As I told Devon, wherever I've gone, I've always enjoyed helping people. And it sounds to me like being an Alpha is about helping."

"It is." Helena looked past Eva to see her son finally coming into the room.

"Mornin' Eva... Mama. Hope there's still food 'cause I'm starvin'." Devon appeared dressed down from the last time she had seen him. He was in his pants and a loose shirt with no shoes with his long dirty blonde hair freshly washed. He held his beads out to his mother.

"Good morning, Devon, I trust you slept well since you are so late." Helena scolded her pup without being overly obnoxious about it. No matter how old they got, she'd always think of him like that. "Get a plate of food before you sit down here." She knew she wouldn't have to say that twice.

Eva was staring right now, and Helena cleared her throat, a sharp brow raised. The girl tried to either cover or refocus by shoveling another few potatoes into her mouth. She'd have to reteach the girl to be a bit more... lady-like? Then again, this wasn't a formal dinner, just a casual family breakfast.

Devon settled in a chair between the two women and began eating.

"Here, Evalyn, let me show you how to fix his braids properly. After the ceremony, it will no longer be my duty to carry it out. Either he does it, or you do it."

"It's symbolic and traditional?" Eva asked as she got up from beside Devon and pushed her chair back out of the way. Her hand went to his shoulder and Devon touched it momentarily and made a rumble in his chest before going back to his eating.

"Yes, the weaving of the beads is a symbolic, nurturing act. You should also know lycan men eat twice what others do. Be sure you prepare for that." Helena spared a giggle there. The mother pulled the brush he offered her through his thick hair. She separated the right half of Devon's hair and sectioned it out for the braids.

"Twice as much? Well, hopefully, we have enough for that," Eva whispered.

"Would you like me to explain the beads and how you should place them, or do you already know this?"

"Mmmm. I know each has meaning. Each about packs, battles, personal ones from mating, and children..."

"Good, then I can just tell you which is what..." Helena made several braids with the hair she had on one side of Devon's head. "You don't always have to follow the same braid pattern, but these beads should be in order. Pack bead is always first, then mate, then children. After those, battles, and awards." As Helena taught and Eva listened, Devon ate.

"Devon has his pack bead now, and beads for his battles, and one for—" She took a pale blue one and held it up.

"That one reminds me of something special. But you can leave it off now." He held his hand out and Helena placed it into his palm. She narrowed her gaze at her son. Apparently, there had been someone special in his life recently for that to be in there. She'd not even paid attention until now. She'd let it go.

"Thank ya, I appreciate it." Devon had accepted his second plate from one of the kitchen staff before both Eva and Helena finished his braids. There was at least half a pound of meat along with at least six scrambled eggs he was now digging into. He glanced up at both women as they finished his hair, and he grinned while licking his lips clean.

"And what do you have planned for the day?" Helena lifted her brow at her son in question.

"I'm gonna take Eva out to practice her shiftin'. If she wants to, that is." His gaze went to Eva, and he smiled at her.

Eva's eyes sparkled in anticipation.

"She's supposed to be fitted this morning for her new clothes." Helena could see the longing between the two and it warmed her heart. "We'll make quick work of your measurements and then you can go. I'll pick out fabrics and see your clothing started. We can choose your ceremony attire this evening."

"I'm not overly picky." Eva finally moved her gaze from Devon to Helena. "I talked about what I like, and I guess the only color I can't wear is yellow. Makes my skin look bad in most light. I trust you, m'lady."

"That's good to know." Helena smiled as she moved around the table with graceful steps. "I'll call the seamstress while the two of you finish your meal." Helena left them then to fetch the lady in question and gave the new lovers their stolen moment.

Pushing his chair back, Devon tugged Eva into his lap with a playful chuckle. "Did ya sleep well? I know I tossed and turned and held myself back from huntin' ya down. I wanted ya in my bed, whether it was to sleep or make love to ya."

"I would've appreciated both. I've gotten adept at resting in unfamiliar territory, at least." She put her hand on his chest and her eyes stared longingly at the skin there, his heartbeat that thumped beneath her touch.

"It won't be unfamiliar for long." Dev nuzzled her jaw and breathed her scent in.

Eva giggled and moved her hands behind his neck to let her fingers roam into his unbraided hair a bit.

"Have ya enjoyed the baths yet? My mama keeps the one below the palace private. After we run, we can enjoy it if ya like." Devon purred a low rumble against the side of her neck as he teased her.

"That sounds wonderful. Are they heated?" she asked, her fingers now moving along his jaw.

"Enough of that in my main hall. Come, Evalyn, and let's get you measured so you can be off with him." Helena summoned Eva from the entry while narrowing her gaze on her son. He knew better, after all.

"Yes, ma'am!" Eva gave him a kiss on the cheek, turned to hop off his lap, and with a bounce to her step, she went after his mother.

Chapter Ten

LEARNING TO BE LYCAN

When next Devon got to see his intended mate, he held a shoulder pack out to her, "Extra clothes for yer shiftin'."

"These clothes your mother insisted on aren't exactly run worthy." She wound up tying the bottom of her skirts to form makeshift pants. Taking the pack, she walked by his side out into the wilderness.

He led her out from the palace and to the north of it, where there were woods and a stream with a spring-fed glen. Their conversation stayed light, Devon sharing about the normal workings of the palace. The structure was beautiful, a lovely stone structure in the middle of a green bunch of fields, surrounded by forests and a lake that was the source of a river nearby. Walking through this was a welcome change.

"Madron Regis kept us near the ocean of water or the sea of sands. I don't think I've ever seen so much green since my old life."

"Well, slavers like ta make sure they stay out along the edges of people's lands. And along the coasts, there are plenty of trade ports available." Devon pointed out. He dropped his pack at the base of a tree and, as Eva did the same, he stripped off his shirt while facing her. Like any warrior, he had his share of scars.

Devon's skin heated slightly. She dropped her pack near his and then stepped closer. He held his hand out to let her know not to get too close.

"Clear yer mind and focus on the wolf. Don't panic and try to hold back, instead go with the feeling and let it guide ya through the shift. It'll be smoother and hurt less. Also, this is difficult enough without clothes. You're wearin' anything takes a lot of mental finesse to incorporate. After all, this ain't just a physical change, but a mental and magical one as well. And any spare items you carry will normally just meld into your wolf-being. But the more you have, the more difficult the shift."

Eva nodded.

"Okay," he took a deep breath, "Like this." Devon closed his eyes and his whole body relaxed and shifted to the big golden brown and white wolf. He stood on all fours and shook his fur out.

"Your markings...your size... Nothing like you exists in my world!"

Devon would have laughed if he weren't shifted. Eva moved her hands over the ridge of his back and walked around him, taking in every detail. They both felt the pull to one another. This time, she took his advice and let it happen.

First, she took off her blouse and her skirt. He wanted her to shift and had shown her how he did it in his own way. He hoped she remembered what he had said. It was a physical and mental...or as many saw it, a magical process. He just had a connection with his wolf that allowed the transformation to be quick and efficient. Eva needed to establish the same connection to her wolf. He sat and watched her.

Instead of shifting from standing, she got to her hands and knees. Then she shook her head as if realizing something. She got to her feet but remained in a crouch. Then she took a deep breath and closed her brown eyes. Within seconds, she changed. Devon got up and huffed as he watched her body slowly adjust to the changes happening within. Eva gasped as the pain ripped through her, but the shifting did not stop. Devon barked and made small lunges, excitedly encouraging his mate.

He was certain the pain was sharp, and she whined, but it was quicker than most would have thought. Once she was in her hybrid form, which was what Senias called a werewolf for some reason, that's when the magic showed through.

The only clothing she had left on her body melted into her fur and got replaced by a pale blonde colored fur. All of her was pale, almost golden colored except her mask and tail, which mixed a darker brown throughout. She was on her four paws. She was shaky at first. Soon enough, Eva was moving all around Devon, still sniffing him and looking him over.

There was a low woof from Dev as he moved around her in slow circles, also catching her scent. She was beautiful in this form as well! He nudged her side with his nose and turned to jog off, then paused. Scratching the ground, he started off again but then paused. He wanted her to see that this part of them wasn't all about breeding or pain. He wanted Eva to run, play, and enjoy her wolf!

She started, then stopped, lifting her front paw tentatively. Eva looked around the woods and then back at him. She made a little growl and woof sound, too. Every step seemed measured and every tree suspect.

Devon noted her caution and paranoia. He'd have to ask her about it later, but he could well imagine that her keepers did not allow this kind of shifting. He ran back to her and nuzzled her face with his own, letting a rumble leave his chest. Then, he took off as he had done before, pausing and looking over his shoulder.

Eva joined him this time, and they both moved through the forest. The momentary fear of retribution was gone. As they ran through the trees, Devon made a game of teaching her to work her wolf. He was showing her how to defend herself and how to take down a larger opponent. Devon spent time this day teaching his mate everything he could. He hoped she enjoyed as many playful moments along the way as she could. Anything that could bring joy while she was in this form would help her find her way through shifting in the future.

By late afternoon, they stretched out on the grass beside the stream. Dev let himself revert to his human form. He was on his stomach in the remnants of his pants, and there, for her to view, were the scars upon his back with their bits of copper glinting from their depths. He didn't move while she inspected his back; the female wolf licking over one scar and then whining.

"They don't hurt when ya touch 'em. If that's what yer wondering." He looked aside. "Can ya shift?" He knew it might be difficult at first. But Eva surprised him by going into it like a pro! She was on her knees at his back immediately. Her palms caressed the skin, and her fingers traced the patterns.

"What happened?" she asked quietly, not stopping her physical connection to him. All her attention was on her mate.

"I was a prisoner during the second war with elves about seventy-five cycles ago now. Being not only a leader to the warriors but also a son to an Alpha made me a target. I didn't complain, because if their attention came to me, then my warriors and the other lycan were safe from their ire."

"I knew someone like you," Eva whispered. She looked at his face. "The coven had those of us who were slaves in the upper areas, and they had slaves made into servants and even lovers. And then there were the fighters. There were some amongst the fighters that tried to get the punishments upon their own shoulders so that the younger ones and the naïve ones didn't take it. I believe some of the younger ones might've broken. They saved those with their strength." Eva motioned toward the markings and then asked, "How long?"

"I was theirs for almost two years and I made sure no lycan died there." Devon rolled to his back so that Eva could stretch out with him. She did so without a second thought and no encouragement. His hand lifted to smooth his fingers partially through her thick, beautiful hair. "I don't hold on to the anger, though. That's too exhausting to hold anger with others. I'm angry and then it's... it's gone."

"That's a good way to be. Anger holds power over you. Keeps you from moving on. But I haven't forgotten, you know? I find that different from holding on to anger. Remembering helps you in the future."

"Well, I figure, if I hold all that anger, pain, and hate towards the elves in me, our Pack will start adopting those same feelings. Not every elf held slaves. And some even fought with us. I don't want those innocent ones getting injured on both sides. Doesn't make me a good example for our people." He wished he could say the same about his father.

"I have met nice elves. One almost bought me before Kieran got there." She moved her face against his upper chest and took in his scent. "She said I would have made a wonderful guardian for her. And I know I would. I know how to fight - as a human. But I prayed she would find someone else. I believed you when you said you would come back for me. I didn't want to go to anyone else."

Devon noticed her hand moving over his chest and then down his muscled abdomen and back. He rumbled deeply from the chest and let his hand move lazily over the skin of her shoulder.

"I made a promise to ya. So even if the elf had bought ya, I would've tracked ya down." Devon would not lie. He was thoroughly enjoying Eva's exploring fingers as they moved across his skin. "I'll keep my hands up here till ya want me to put 'em somewhere else." Devon brought his hands up and tucked them beneath his head. There was a relaxed, pleasant chuckle from the big lycan as he lay there watching his mate. Devon couldn't help but wonder if she'd ever gotten such freedom with the men in the coven. If not, they were even more horrible than he already thought, and he hoped the Goddess visited fits on them.

"You're my mate. I don't mind if you put your hands on me, Devon. There may be times when I don't want to be sexual with you because of pain or something... and I'll let you know. I promise. But know that I always want to touch you and feel you. If I didn't want that, I wouldn't be here." She got up and straddled him just to let him know for sure that she was serious. "And as of right now, I definitely want to be sexual with you."

Right then, the only person on his mind was straddling his hips. His golden gaze lit up and that deep rumble moved through his chest for Eva. Devon's hands left their place beneath his head and moved up Eva's thighs. His calloused fingers moved over her supple skin and then vanished beneath the material of her bloomers.

"I just never want ya to fear my touch. I will always be as gentle or as rough as ya want me to be." Devon moved her so that her heated center rubbed against the hard ridge within his pants. He didn't want to go too far, too fast. He wanted to thoroughly enjoy their first time together.

She looked down at where they nearly connected with surprise. She rocked against him, her scent hitting the surrounding air. "Devon..."

"By the Goddess, Eva, ya feel so good! Come here to me, my mate, and kiss me."

Chapter Eleven

COMMUNICATION OR CONFRONTATION

KIERAN CAME OUT OF the bathing room in his palace suite with a towel at his waist and one moving through his still-matted hair. He really needed to get hold of the mess. But he had more important matters to attend to. Hearing the lock click on the door, he turned around to face his mate.

"If you need the room, just give me time to get clothes on."

"I'm here to make sure your hair is proper, and I braid the beads in." Helena took the seat from the vanity and placed it in the middle of the floor.

The big Alpha looked back over his shoulder as if thinking she was talking to someone else. But there wasn't anybody there. He turned back to her and cocked his head slightly, much like a wolf that had heard something he couldn't believe.

"Oh, don't get started!" She slapped the seat of the chair. "I am trying to run a proper household here to give Eva the proper teachings of being a mate to our son. How am I supposed to do that if I'm not handling my own mate?"

"I suppose ..." Kieran stepped over to the seat and took it, waiting for the pain to begin. Just because she knew how to handle the hair, didn't mean she'd be going easy on him. "My beads are in the box on the dresser."

"I know. You've kept them there when not wearing them for all our lives together. If you ever changed a bit, it would surprise me."

"Am I being scolded or are you just...t...owwww!" Kieran thought she was about to pull his hair right off his head when she hit a mat. "Damn, woman,

I've been in the field all this time! Ya think I've got time or energy ta keep my hair up? Get some oil or go easy."

"I figured you might have one of your whores handle that, considering they get the pleasure of the other end well enough."

Kieran stiffened while Helena stepped to the bathroom to get the oil to help with the tangles. He took a deep breath and let it out slowly at least five times before saying a word.

"It's not like I got someone warmin' this bed up for me. So, I take what's offered."

"Let's not fight…" Helena returned to stand behind him once more. She rubbed some of the oil onto her hands and then into his hair before beginning to work the tangles out.

"You're the one who brought it up, mate."

It was her turn to take a deep breath in and let it out slowly. She worked in the first braid. "You're right, I did." Helena focused on her task for a moment. "All I'm saying is to at least do your whoring away from those we know." She started on the second braid after having placed the beads on the first one. "If not for my sake, at least for that of our children."

"They're not children anymore. They'll always be my pups, but they're adults. And I doubt any of 'em know a damn thing about our arrangements. I promised you I'd keep it that way. I ain't about to break that promise."

"Shame and embarrass me all you want, Kieran, but they shouldn't." Helena set the next bead. Kieran noticed her hands shook a little as she began the third braid.

"What do ya want from me? I won't be celibate anymore for ya to…" He noticed someone at the door, and sniffing the air, told him it was his dragon. "Look, I'll not speak if we can't be civil."

After finishing the rest of the braids and beading them, Helena worked the knots out of the rest of his hair and moved her hand over it. Kieran stood up and looked in the mirror. He looked a lot better than he had in a very long while.

"Have I not been a fit mate to you? I've given you sons and a daughter. I attend to your home and ensure all is well while you are out fighting and warring. Is that not enough to at least garner the right to some respect? And yet you make me a laughingstock. You shame and humiliate me by whoring right here in our home?" She was whispering, her eyes pleading. "I'm not blind and neither is anyone else here at the palace or in the village. The maids? Really?"

"I've not fucked a maid in man a year, Helena. Where are you getting this?" Kieran huffed.

"The scent of your dirty clothes," Helena looked to the pile in the corner and then back at him. "Shall I go fetch her right this minute and ask her?"

He growled, and his eyes shimmered. "Don't punish someone that'll keep quiet. She's got as much ta lose as you. She won't challenge ya. And it wasn't here. I'll burn the clothes by fire if ya need it." He caught her arm gently before she tugged it away. "I swear to the Goddess it wasn't here."

He looked to the door, "Senias, stop lurking and bring yer ass on in."

Helena's cheeks became rosy red. She turned away from them both and began furiously cleaning up the mess she'd made in helping with his wild mane.

"What's happening, Scales? You got my daily report?" Kieran grabbed the reed basket that stood at the side of the restroom suite and shoved his dirty clothes into it.

"Derek's taken to Rory. I think that's a good idea, to be honest. The boy's going to need a lot of help to come out of what he was witness to," Senias said as he walked into the door. He bowed to Helena, who bowed slightly in return. "The scouts have followed the elves past the Blue Ridge. They've camped in the area."

"Then we know where to strike, don't we?" Kieran's growling response had the dragon backing up a step. He wanted to keep the creature where he should be, and the slight movement told the Alpha that was still possible. He expected a fuss from Sen. After all, he and Inea had already been trying to pull back a little in every battle. Inea's injuries last time they dealt with anything the elves had done bothered them all.

"You're not seriously considering going after the elves again, are you?" Helena's hands were on her hips. "Devon and Eva are to be mated. We are to have everyone in the pack here for the first time in years for this full moon ceremony. I have arranged for other pack dignitaries as guests. You said this last battle was actually the last battle. Kieran, you promised!"

"I promised to keep you and our pups and the pack safe..."

"And you've gotten two killed, one captured, and who knows how much danger you've put Gareth into!" The growl from her chest was loud and pronounced. She turned to the draconic man. "Are the elves a threat? Are they leaving the lands near ours?"

"Well, I'm not sure how much of a threat they are. If I go by what I've seen previously, it looks like they know they're done. They're taking everything with them and moving slowly back northwest to their own city-state of Calen."

"You know that can change at the drop of a paw," Kieran couldn't believe he was arguing this. "I'm not sayin' ya don't have the celebration. I'm sayin' we be prepared with defense, and we make sure and push 'em the rest of the way on out to Calen before risking anything more. If that pushes the ceremony and celebration off by a moon, at least everybody's safe."

"This pack...every pack...needs some normalcy, Kieran. Their Alpha is back, and the warriors are back, and you'll have them turn right around and take those risks again? They will not be happy and there will be challenges to your place - to our place."

"Maybe...but I'll face 'em to be sure everybody's safe." Kieran had handled challengers before and had no issues doing it again.

"You're not making sure everyone is safe. With every battle, more of our pack gets lost. It's the cost of war and I know it all too well. Stop warmongering. Let our pack just live!"

"Since when did ya become part of my inner circle of advisors, Helena? How much experience do you have in strategy? Did ya forget ta tell me about all that before?" Kieran growled, his arms crossing over his chest.

"Considering I've had to run this pack in your absence, I've lost pups, and I must help people through their losses to these wars? I believe I should get some bit of a say!"

Senias moved his gaze back and forth between the two Alphas. Both were growling by the time the dragon cleared his throat. When they turned their attention to him, he took the chance to explain something.

"Inea and I have not been faring well. Our control has been waning recently. We've also been in pain from the limitations on our bonds - bonds we had before coming here. My suggestion would be to keep an eye on the elves but let them go. Don't take a battle to them."

"You know how spiteful those creatures are, Senias. You really think this is over?" Kieran turned from the two and paced to the side of the bedroom, a hand moving through the loose side of his hair. His eyes were cold as he turned back to the dragon. "We need ta drive 'em all the way to their own damned land is what we need ta do."

"That'd take months. You think you should put things off for months when we already know the elves are on the move? Life goes on, Kieran. Just have scouts go back to look around and ensure the elves are still moving northward before and then after the ceremony. If they are, let them. If they aren't, then you plan a little encouragement." Senias waited, Helena as well. "I don't want to be pulled into another battle. Nor does anyone else."

Kieran took a deep breath and let it out, his nose flaring before his amber eyes took in the united front of the two waiting. It was a compromise. The big Alpha growled deeply and nodded, but he grabbed his filthy clothes and made his way out of the room before either said more.

He'd need to burn the clothes, and the chore got him away. So far as he could tell, Senias hadn't caught on. They didn't just smell of the frisky maid he'd enjoyed late in the night. Had Helena any sense of battle and the smells of the field, she might have noticed the smell of blood. Kieran could at least guarantee one group of elves that had camped closer to his lover's village would never attack the lycan again.

Chapter Twelve

MATES CAN'T HELP IT

UNAWARE OF THE DRAMA unfolding at the old palace his family kept, Devon had his soon-to-be official mate straddling his body. After they had run through the forest and he had gotten her to shift without hesitation, they had found themselves like this, slowly exploring.

Eva didn't hesitate to kiss him. Running around in their wolf forms had only made them wilder and more needy. She kissed him with a roughness born of inexperience. Eva wanted him, and she wanted to feel good with him. And she definitely knew how to accomplish that on a practical level. So, his inaction confused the hell out of her!

"Why are you waiting?" she asked breathlessly against his lips and chin as she nipped him. Then she sat up, her hands moving from his chest to her own hips. She still moved against his hardness a little to keep that tinge of pleasure there, but her stance showed some annoyance.

"Easy, beautiful, I don't want to rush this." He moved one hand down to the front of Eva's body until he reached the soft curls that covered her core. "I don't want to rush at making love to ya, my mate. I could hurt ya if I did." His thumb slid into that sweet warm spot, and he rubbed it against the pearl hidden there. "My pleasure will come with yours."

"But...." She closed her eyes when she realized what he was doing. Her eyes fluttered to close as her mind concentrated on the physical enjoyment. Eva had a tough time thinking about what she meant to say. Her body rubbed against his with more force once he found her pleasure place. She whined and lost her breath.

"How... together...how...if.... if...." and with the last 'if' she cried out and shook with her first climax... and they hadn't even joined yet! The front of his pants dampened quickly. She shoved his hand away and turned from him quickly, whining. She had to catch her breath, too! How had he done that so well?

"Let me show you." Devon licked his battered lips and could still taste Eva on them from her rough onslaught.

"It's just...I...I've felt something like that, but not...not quite as good."

"So inexperienced in actual love-makin'? I hate people treated ya so wrong. But I aim ta set things straight with yer mind, yer body, and yer soul," Devon whispered. "I'll always make sure yer well taken care of before I see ta myself."

"Not all of them were bad." She swallowed. "But, I don't want to think about them." Eva once again kissed him as if they'd never have this chance again. So he disengaged.

"No... don't rush." Devon rumbled for her and waited til their gazes met. Then he slowly took her mouth again. He moved his tongue along her bottom lip and softly grazed his canines over its fullness before dipping his tongue in to move against hers.

She blushed a bit and wondered if she should apologize, but the way Devon taught her and didn't punish her? Eva had not experienced this. She did her best to emulate what he had just shown her. She wanted him to feel as good as he made her feel.

Ending the kiss, Devon placed his mouth on Eva's ear and growled, "Ya smell delicious, and I wanna taste."

"Taste?" She was in a daze when he said such, and her mind wandered back to her past. What did he mean by - taste? So far, he had surprised her with every turn. She hoped he would pleasantly surprise her again.

"Whoop!" Eva couldn't help the sound as Devon rolled them over so that Eva was lying beneath him. With a villainous grin on his handsome face, the big lycan slid down Eva's body. He paused a moment at her breasts to tease each nipple through the material, leaving damp patches before he moved down to her stomach. He pressed a kiss at her navel, then he removed her panties. "Spread yer legs, sweetness. Let me get ya a little closer to the stars."

Eva bit her lip and slowly spread her legs. She wasn't used to someone being down there. And coming from a vampire coven, the term 'tasting' had a completely different meaning for her.

Devon dropped to his elbows and placed his face right at her center. He leaned in and ran his tongue over her damp nether lips before parting them to find her clit and suck on it. He rumbled and licked and feasted.

Eva went from gasping to groaning to giggling to panting to having to move her damned body to get him to stop! She'd never felt so much pleasure before and soon, Devon couldn't even move without her sucking in a breath. He went to it deeper now, leaving her sensitive little nub alone. But this time it was like he had found the perfect pressures and rhythm. Finally, she reached down and moved her fingers lightly over her own clit while he continued licking in that perfect spot. The sounds she made were instinctual. She did not know where they were coming from!

She opened herself up more and groaned when he sped up but in the same place. This time, when she came, her legs moved inward with the spasm, and she was glad he had placed his shoulders where he had. Otherwise, he would've wound up with a headache!

"No, Dev.... st... stop..." She was shivering again, sweat glittering off of her body from the pure effort of the orgasm. Her ears were ringing, and her legs were shaking.

"Then it's perfect time." It was while she was in the middle of this intense pleasure that he stopped his tongue play and released himself from the ruined pants. Eva caught his gaze as he slid the first few inches in. He groaned roughly and had to pause midway. She wondered why. "Slow, remember? This time we go slow. We get to the stars this time... together."

Her stare was incredulous, to be sure, but she nodded. Eva would try. She hitched her hips once, accidentally. She was trying not to go overboard. But as he pushed further, she growled.

"Why? Why are we holding back? Both... want this..." She felt her hips hitch upon him again and she grabbed at his shoulders, urging him onward with a needy whine. She wanted to feel him. Even now, her inner muscles were spasming against his girth, and she was fighting it as best she could.

Devon's control slipped a little, and as he pushed the rest of the way, he growled deeply. The way she grabbed and demanded more made Devon's wolf want to break free. His eyes glittered as he withdrew and thrust again.

"Because my wolf wants to claim ya and that can't happen... yet... the ceremony... comes first."

As Eva's inner muscles tightened, he groaned, and his thrust sped up. As one arm balanced Devon above his lover, his other hand grabbed her thigh and lifted her leg to shift the angle. His muscles bulged as he worked them both. He dropped to kiss her and urged her to move as she wanted; to touch him as she desired. She could rip him to shreds with her nails and he wouldn't have cared!

Eva's hands were over one shoulder and under the other. When he got to a certain angle and rhythm, she whimpered and lifted herself to meet his thrusts even more. Her nails bit into him. Soon she was moving with wild abandon. And this time, she arched her back and actually howled.

Devon was right there with her. His entire body tightened, and he flexed several times. He thrust until his body was spent. That's when he rolled carefully to his back with Eva held tight to him. She wasn't sure how long they were like this, but she loved feeling his cock still inside of her. Her body went off again thanks to that. The orgasm wasn't as strong, but it felt amazing.

"Ceremony?" Eva whispered as she tried to catch her breath. "Please tell me... we don't have to... you know... mate... in front of people?" Eva was trying to catch her breath. What did he mean they had to wait for the ceremony?

There was a pause, and his brows furrowed.

"In some traditions, the new couple must prove they've mated. I...I don't know your culture, Devon. I need to know." She held her breath.

"Oh," Dev had a rough chuckle. "No love, that is just for us alone, but when I take ya as my mate, our scents mingle forever, and when yer around others, they'll know who yer mated to." Devon nuzzled her and rumbled gently from his chest.

Eva took a deep breath, and her body relaxed. "You said we had to wait for the ceremony for your wolf to claim mine. I was worried."

"Sweetheart, I ain't sharing you with anybody else. The ceremony is about words and tradition, nothing more."

"Thank the Goddess!"

Chapter Thirteen

FRIEND OF A DRAGON

"So, what else did ya like today?"

"Mmmm…" She forced herself up to better look into his eyes. "To run with you. It made my shifting to my wolf so much easier than I've ever experienced."

Pressing a kiss to her lips, Devon almost purred the rumble was so deep and low. "I want ya to run with me, too. Every chance we get."

"So, who else should I know?" she asked before settling back in against him. "And what else? I know I'm bound to embarrass both of us before I get how things work here. But if you tell me things, maybe I can be less embarrassed. Maybe…" she giggled.

"I think ya gonna do just fine. Mama can be stern, but she means well. She'll show ya everything ya need, I promise. As for embarrassing me, I ain't too worried about that. Just stay close and watch us. There are some things that are gonna stand out. Our mates do little things. I mean, the ones that follow traditions. My mama serves my ole man before she serves herself and, being Alpha, he always gets served first. Some mates share plates and when yer carrying our pups, I'll serve or feed ya from my plate. I'll always make sure yer taken care of first."

"I don't see why I can't do that. Besides, one thing I know about is cooking. Since you eat so much, I'll be happy to cook and serve your food. I'll have to dust off the memories of all those recipes I learned when I was younger. What else?"

"We ain't keen on a lot of clothes and hardly wear shoes unless it's necessary." He caressed his hand down her spine. "There's full moon ceremonies where couples get mated and births or carrying pups get announced." Devon smoothed his fingers over her curls. He loved the texture of her hair. It was so soft and gorgeous. Kind of like her, he mused to himself.

Clearing his throat, as if she could hear his thoughts, he continued, "Yer a healer, so you're gonna want to spend time with our shaman to learn their ways. They know a lot about herbs and medicinal things. They'll teach ya the seasons, the holidays, and their prayers. I can't teach ya any of that except maybe a couple of prayers and the basic stuff about our holidays."

"I want that very much." Eva closed her eyes as he moved his fingers through her hair. She was relaxing more.

"One thing I need to take ya to visit is the Great Oak. That's where our dead rest, or at least stones for them, do."

"Memorials?" she asked quietly.

"Yes, I guess ya could call it that. My brothers have stones out there and we can go see 'em. We lost them in the first war with the elves."

"Do you think these wars with the elves are almost done?"

Devon drew in a deep breath and let it out slowly. He knew the idea of finding the one she was supposed to be with only to lose him to yet another war worried her. That was plain as day.

"I pray that this is our last war with them. There've been fewer lycan lost in this war. It's my thought that they understand we're no longer born to be slaves to them, vampires, or dragons." The sound of wind rushing through the nearby trees told Devon that a certain dragon had come in for a landing. The sound was close enough to make Eva jump and sit up to attention, looking around.

"What's that?"

"Relax, Eva, it's only Senias. He's known to my Pack. You somewhat met him before. Maybe not officially. He and his dragoness have helped us through this war." Setting her aside gently, Devon climbed to his feet and then helped Eva to hers. "Come on, I'll introduce ya." Devon fastened his belt back in place and waited, so she had her underwear in place before continuing.

"I saw him... at the other pack's keep... the dark one?"

Devon could tell that this walk had Eva back to being very cautious again. Her eyes were dashing over the trail ahead, and her hand squeezed his. They backtracked and came across the clothes she needed, and he picked up his shirt. The couple cleared the woods, and it was only then that the dragon came into view.

Senias was a magnificent sight to eyes that were accustomed to him, and so Devon could only imagine what a sight he made to Eva. The horn-like protrusions around the face and over the back of the head made him intimidating, along with his size. The scales were dark in color, black in some places, but the light glinting off his leather skin and scales showed otherwise. There were browns and maroons to deep reds swirled in patterns all over the dragon.

He was drinking from the stream that ran through their lands and fed the large lake from which they got fresh water. When he noted the two lycan, his enormous head raised up, and he shook off the excess water before his tongue moved over the edging of his hard mouth.

"Senias, shift and come meet my mate-to-be. I'll introduce ya properly, my friend." While Sen spent more time with the Alpha, Dev still felt they had become friends over the years.

~ She seems quite pleased to be in awe of my magnificence as I am, Devon, ~ Senias chuckled at the way the girl was staring at him. The dragon's chuckle came across as a deep sound, indeed. He moved forward, his wingtips grasping the large boughs of the trees nearby. His blue-green eyes focused on further study of the woman. The dragon stopped pushing his mindspeak only to Devon and shared the conversation. ~ Good on the eyes, am I? ~ He bared his teeth in a smile that might have most people running.

"You speak to our minds?" she asked, almost in awe of what she'd just experienced.

~ I just did, yes. ~ Another chuckle rumbled the ground as he bent forward, chest to the grass.

"That's brilliant! I've not had anyone mindspeak to me since the vampires."

~ Vampires? You know of vampires? ~ The dragon made a low-frequency sound that shook their bodies to the bone. ~ In this world or the other? ~

"The other. Coven called Eriksson. But they aren't as nice with their mindspeak as you are. They don't care if it gives you a headache. I don't feel that with you. And yes, you are gorgeous to look at, now that I know you won't eat me!"

~ Never said I wouldn't eat you. ~ He snapped his jaws a few feet in front of them and again, the vibrating sound came from the gigantic creature and an obvious chuckle.

"Oh, he isn't full of himself and cocky at all." Devon was grinning when he winked at Eva before looking back up at Sen.

~ I'm not cocky, I'm honest. ~ He huffed warm air over both before the flash of magic left them momentarily blinded. When they could see again, the human form of the dragon stood before them, only some light silken pants on. Those hung low on his waist, tied with a red sash. His hair looked almost brown, but the shimmer from the sun showed reddish strands and highlights throughout. He was tall, but not as large or tall as Devon.

"I would continue to speak in such a way, but I know Devon hates mind-speak. I don't want to give you a headache, prince. Seems your mate has no trouble with it. Perhaps she could've been kindred in another life?" The girl was still staring. Senias raised a brow. "This is our official introduction, isn't it? Senias of Morias. And you might be...?"

"Eva La Croix, soon to be Weylyn," she held her hand out to him. The draconic man took her hand gently, and he kissed the back of it appropriately.

Devon raised a brow.

"Oh, traditional and proper. How nice. You definitely are from the other side."

"Mmmhmm.."

Eva watched him, staring. The dragon smiled at the way she did so, but Devon didn't seem overly pleased by it. So Senias put his hand between them and snapped his fingers, breaking her trance.

"You need to eat," she whispered. "I could cook a meal made by my mother, my grandmother for you both, and we could all talk."

The draconic man's head canted as if he were still in his dragon form. It was almost a cat-like movement that spoke of curiosity. "Where the hell did you find this one?" Senias chuckled. "She has the sight. Or she has good assumptions."

Eva placed her freed hand on Devon's upper arm. He wasn't sure what to make of Eva's reactions. She wanted to feed the dragon? Was it a concern for the dragon's needs or something else?

Senias, bless him, took a couple of steps back from her and Devon took notice. But the dragon kept jovial about the meeting. "I admit, I'm a lot leaner than I was when I first came over, but we've been at war, lady Eva. Was bound to happen. My human form is just that. Human. I'll never be as big as your mate."

"Yes, but you seem unwell to me. Why did you come here?"

"People who believe in hell. They came after all my kind. We're the monsters in their stories," Senias explained.

"So, I remember. But you're no monster. And you're not doing well here in this world." There was a long, uncomfortable pause as the dragon regarded her and what she had said.

"You found yourself a hedge witch from the other world?" Senias asked Devon, but his eyes remained on Eva.

"Don't matter what she is. I took one look at her and wanted no other. Perhaps one day yer true mate will cross yer path and I bet ya get my meaning then."

Senias had shared little about his life prior to coming through and joining up with them. Dev only knew of his current dragon "mate" and the lycan knew they weren't exactly monogamous.

"But if he has a mate, why...?" Eva was confused and she was also nervous about how to finish that line of questioning.

"Mmmm... sorry. Dragons do not see mates the same as lycan." Senias whispered, his fingers moving roughly through his reddish hair. "We are partners and trust one another—"

"You love her, but you love her as a platonic love?" Eva asked. The draconic man nodded. "When you were helping her at the other packlands, I noticed."

"Besides, Sen prefers men, though the occasional woman ends up in his bed." Devon gave a wolfish grin.

"I have no trouble including them in the fun." The dragon smirked. "The problem with women is that they can get with child. And I would never wish to visit a child such as I would create on an unsuspecting woman."

Devon respected the dragon for learning their ways.

Senias bounced his shoulders. "And Devon's correct in that I fancy the feel of hard muscle and the scent of a man. I'm afraid such isn't the norm in either world. Over here, I don't give a damn. However, if an interested woman is as beautiful as your mate—"

Eva didn't smile, but she blushed.

"I don't share." Devon took Eva's hand in his own, just to further illustrate the point. "Eva says you need food. What does my ole man have ya doin' today that has you starving yerself?"

"Actually, I'm out here because he says I'm going to take a break. And Nea said to walk away from the palace. And your mate says I need to eat. So, I suppose I'm trying to do all the above." Senias took a deep, huffing breath.

"In that case, why don't we all shift and go hunting?" Devon looked from his friend to his mate. "I wanted to show Eva how to hunt in her wolf form anyways. So why not now?" The way Dev figured it, this would knock several things out at once.

"What do you want me to do? I could... herd some of the low deer your way?" Senias offered. "Maybe we could teach her wind shifts and tracking and then that? Where would you like to begin?" Senias' blue-green eyes seemed to dance with mischief.

"Anything the both of you want to help me with would be fine. But I think I'd like to get bathed before we go too far."

Devon's love reminded him she wasn't really wearing much of anything. And though he liked the smell of sex and grass on her, maybe that wasn't something that should remain so...fragrant? He nodded, another wolfish grin sprouting. "We just need ta get our bags and then we can go to the baths I told ya about back home."

"I know a wonderful, private spot further up along the ridge. I can fly you both to it. Otherwise, it'd be tricky." Senias looked between the two. "The water's actually a little warmer because of the midday sun hitting the stone."

"If it's out here, it'd waste less time and flying? You'd let us fly with you?" When the draconic man nodded, Eva turned to look at Devon and she mouthed, "Yes... please..."

"Guess we'll take ya up on that offer." Dev rushed to the tree nearby where they had left their packs to grab them up.

Senias smiled brightly before moving off from Eva enough that his gigantic body wouldn't hurt her when it popped into existence. The dragon shifted immediately. Senias offered to gather them in his claws to take them for the ride. It would be more fun for the lady.

"Thank ya for this, Sen!" When Devon returned, he helped Eva into Sen's claw and climbed behind her.

Chapter Fourteen

DRAGONS NEED LOVE, TOO

THE FLYING WOULD SOON begin. The gigantic dragon was trying to decide what would be the best, safest takeoff. He was very careful with his friends. The climb would be slower and more strenuous for him, but it was obvious to Devon that the dragon meant to beat his wings and move up the side of the mountain.

~ It's good to get time with ya away from my ole man. I like time with ya that doesn't involve battles. ~

~ You do? ~ The mind speak bounced back from the dragon.

Sen flapped his wings and was taking them up along the rocky area of the hills before moving toward the treeline. Just as Devon figured, the dragon was being safe. It was exhausting, but Devon preferred safety for his mate to showing off.

~ Yeah, why wouldn't I? ~

~ I suppose I assume people don't enjoy being around me. Unless we're all partying and drinking. I tend to be the life of the party and that makes it all fun. ~

Devon held Eva to him and kissed the shell of her ear. ~ Well, I don't see ya as just there for parties and battles. I've been happy ta call you a friend for a while now. I try to include ya whenever I can. Ya just happen ta be with my father a lot. ~

~ I'm honored you trust me, to be a friend. ~ Senias felt thrilled about the realization. ~ I suppose I wasn't sure anyone really saw me as friendship material. ~

~This is how much I trust ya - I'm mind speakin' ya and I don't nor-mally do that. And yer carryin' my future in your claws. ~ Eva held Devon tighter once they were climbing further into the hills. The waterfalls and the coniferous trees made this part of the packlands different, but it was still pleasing to the eyes and even more so to the nose.

Once he'd found the clear-water lake made from run-off, the dragon let his back claws hit the ground. Gently, he lowered his front-clawed hands and opened them. They were on an enormous boulder that was mostly covered by the surrounding soil and moss, making it much like a flat stone floor. A portion of it jutted out into the clear, fresh water of a small lake.

At most, the water was only as high as Eva was tall. But it was shallow on one side and deeper on the other. On the deeper side, the ground went into a normal rounded river stone where the stream met this bypass. The water was so clear one could see every colorful stone. The dragons had been enjoying this little spot since they got to the packlands. It was obvious they had cleared the land just enough to allow for comfortable landings and wrestling. The dragons spared the rest of the treeline to keep eyes from seeing into the nicer area.

Senias moved away from the lycan couple toward the other stone.

"Oh, my... a ride with a dragon and then this? It's gorgeous!" Eva let Devon help her down, and she turned in a spin as she took in all the natural beauty around them.

"You're welcome. I'm glad you like it," Senias spoke because he had shifted. He sat on the upper stone, looking in the opposite direction. He knew proper manners. And he knew when to use them. It was when he didn't respect someone that he didn't give a fuck.

Eva giggled as she took the clothes Devon offered her from the bag and placed them on the dry stone so the sun could warm them. Then she removed the rest of her dirty clothes before walking into the water. Devon was right behind. The dragon had been correct. The water was warmer than the stream water. She quickly made her way to sit where she could.

"Tu es de quelle partie du monde?" Senias asked.

"Je suis d'Haïti," Eva's eyes got large, she smiled more brightly and looked to the man. "You're French?"

"Nope. But I've lived in France for a long time. I noticed your accent." He absently moved his fingers on the stone.

As Sen and Eva spoke in an unfamiliar tongue, Devon washed himself up. He wasn't upset, nor did he demand that they speak in a familiar language. No need. Besides, the sound of it was nice to the ears, for sure.

"Well, if we get some fish or deer today, I will make you some fine spicy Haitian cuisine. Maybe it'd make you feel better?" Eva watched the draconic man from afar.

"You know, the way to both a Lycan's heart and a Dragon's heart is through the stomach. So, maybe I would be in a better mood after such." Senias stretched and moved to lie back so he could soak up more of the sun.

Eva whispered in Devon's ear, "Your friend, he's ... very sad." She hugged her mate and added, "His aura always been so dark? He doesn't seem the type to hold such in his soul. It's like the anger we spoke of earlier when you told me about your scars. There is darkness around his soul."

"I wouldn't know Eva. I can't see his aura, remember? That's your gift, not mine. But if he's sad, I'm sure it'll pass. We'll keep him company and busy until it does, hmmm?" Devon hugged her back even as he cast a concerned gaze toward his friend. He heard her clear her throat and when he met her gaze, Eva motioned toward where Senias was lying.

"When you speak to him, you make his darkness into light," she whispered.

Was this what it was like having a mate? Actually, having to do things you planned to do - but having to do them right then and there?

With a sigh, he nodded, and soon, he waded out of the water and tugged on his fresh pants. He didn't bother with a shirt since they'd be hunting soon. Making his way to the shifted dragon, he cleared his throat with a rumble that had the auburn-haired man turning his head toward him.

"You alright?"

"I think so. Why?" Senias replied easily enough.

"Seems like you got a lot on your mind, and I'm a pretty good listener."

"You're usually off with your boys, drinking and prowling. Why should the things that fill a dragon's mind bother you?" Sen lifted himself up to sit again and pulled his bare feet up to bend his knees.

There was a big sigh from Devon when he crouched down beside Sen. "Because all of that doesn't matter. You seem damn distant even by standards already set. I walked in on something the other day in my ole man's office. Have anything to do with that? You're my friend and I'm here for you when you need me—so start talkin'."

"I feel the pull of the other world. My world." Senias took a breath. "And the lover that I left there. Sebastian."

The rush of air that left Sen's lips, the way he looked at the stone beneath them? Devon knew those expressions. He said nothing.

"I came here to flee those hunting me, to keep them from finding my friends and my lover. The hunters would have taken me in and then Crimson and their Council would inevitably charge anyone I knew with crimes for aiding me. So, I came here, where I wound up finding friends in need. I remain to help you all. Inea and I didn't leave by our own desires, Devon. Crimson was dead set on turning the world against us and letting hunters finish it all off. They were culling all of us. But it's been years since we crossed over. And we're homesick."

"Ya wanna go back to this Sebastian and she wants to go back to her kindred? So… that's one thing. But that's not new, is it? What does that have ta do with being told to leave the palace and being in such a snit?" Devon was trying to understand.

"Inea shooed me from the palace because she worries about me dealing with that boy we rescued." He sighed. "I hope you and your mate never lose a child. It rips your heart apart. And when you find others in need and hurting, well, that pain comes back. It haunts me still, losing our kitling. I suppose it haunts Inea, too. But she's much stronger than I am."

The mention of Rory saddened Devon as he listened to his friend explain the situation with Inea. So, they had lost a child between them? He was learning a lot in one sitting. No wonder Eva said Senias was dark, or that something was wrong with his aura. He doubted that the dragon had said anything about this to anyone. There were people all around the dragon, happy for his protection, for what he could provide…and not one of them realized how lonely this was for him.

"You were mates and yet, yer in different beds with different people all the time. Sometimes it's hard for me ta remember you might've had children." Devon looked back over his shoulder to Eva, who was swimming and washing in the warm pool. He couldn't imagine being with anyone else at this point. And they'd only just met.

"Some dragons mate, as you lycan do. But most of us? When our needing hits us, we rut, and we hopefully make a kitling. I love my kindred in the way you love your Eva. For me, it's Sebastian. For her, it's been Seamus for years. Now? I think she may also fancy your brother."

"And Sebastian is on the other side, waiting for ya?" Devon asked.

"I hope he is. We haven't communicated. Neither of us knew where the other would land. All I know is what city he planned to meet me in." Senias took another deep breath. "It's not just that we miss our kindred, Devon. To be honest, I feel more and more lost on this side the longer I stay. I think maybe I should go back, rejoin Sebastian with a new name and identity, and enjoy life for as long as life allows." He smirked and hit Devon's knee with the back of his hand. "Why should you get all the fun? Besides, you've driven the elves out of all the pack lands. This last slaughter? The one we found in the Rourke packlands? It was a parting fuck-you, to be sure. They won't be back."

"I hope yer right, cause I want these lands safe for my mate and our future pups." Devon glanced towards Eva, enjoying the water, and then back at Sen. "Have ya told the ole man yet?"

"The other reason I needed to leave the palace. My patience with him is short. He keeps coming up with more to do. I've told him my reaction to things hasn't been safe as of late. He wanted me to rest instead of helping with the pulling in of the scouts or asking me to watch the perimeter. So, maybe he sees it, too? Maybe he knows and just isn't saying it."

Broad shoulders shrugged. "Maybe he does. I know he won't be happy that yer leaving. He's gonna try to stop ya. Are you ready for that? I'll have yer back, Senias, if it's the thing you need ta do. I'll miss ya, but if you need this, you need it."

"Stopping us from leaving would be a bad idea. If my mind is this muddled, and I'm relaxed? Well, I'd hate to become irrational." His blue-green gaze rested on Devon. "A lycan who has lost to his wolf is nothing compared to a dragon who no longer recognizes friend from foe." Senias turned to watch Eva as she went into the deeper water. "I would never want to place you or your mate in danger."

Just the idea of a dragon who was out of control chilled Devon to the bone. .

"I can understand that, and I'm grateful. Because I never wanna see ya that way. Are ya gonna stay for our full moon ceremony, or ya planning to leave before that?" Devon asked as he stood to stretch his long legs out.

"I wouldn't want to miss your ceremony. That is if I'm invited."

"Of course, you and Nea are invited! It wouldn't be as great if ya weren't there, my friend." Devon's grin faded a little. "Just don't get lost and forget yer way back Sen. I want ta see you again and know how things work out. Even if it's just for a visit by all of ya and I'm including yer Sebastian in that."

"I'm not sure Sebastian would like the weather here. And I'm not sure Kieran would like Sebastian." Senias chuckled at the thought of the two meeting. Both were very dominant in their personalities.

"I mean, he must be pretty important to ya. I'd like to meet him someday. Perhaps we'll be good friends too."

"That would be nice." Senias smiled. "We've given up so very much for one another. The pull I feel for him? It frightens me. But it also excites me."

Devon rested a hand on Sen's shoulder, and his accent dropped away.

"No matter how long it takes for you to return, our door is always open to you. You're always going to have a hot meal and a warm bed in my house, Senias of Morias. I know you don't understand why and probably won't for several years to come, but I count you amongst my dearest and closest friends. We are always here for you."

"Thank you, Devon." Rising to his feet, Senias stretched with a groan. Devon joined him.

"Now, let's show my mate how to hunt proper and get bloodied the right way. Then we can enjoy some good alc at the fires while the meat cooks or as Eva cooks it, her way for us. And of course, that means we get another bathing time." Devon looked pointedly toward his mate. "Next time we bathe - alone?"

"If we're allowed. Your mother is very proper and strict." Eva slowly stood and made her way out, unashamed by her nakedness, before grabbing up her already dirty, over-large shirt. "But I'll definitely cook you up some goodness from recipes I love."

"Mmmm... sounds good to me. But you both need to be ready. When I hunt, I go for a large quantity... we'll be feeding the pack." Senias walked forward and shifted to his dragon form once again. He stretched languidly, snapping and popping sinew and bone. ~ You know that goes both ways, yes? If you need anything, and I'm not here, get me word. I will always help you, Devon. ~ Senias mind spoke to his friend; a friend who had now impressed upon him something much deeper than he had originally thought was there.

When the dragon took off, he turned to look at his soon-to-be mate. She was watching the big black and maroon dragon take to the air.

"You know, you are very good for him." Eva hugged him and kissed his cheek.

"Oh, is that so?"

"Yes." She smiled. "You help make his darkness into light."

CHAPTER FIFTEEN

HEARTACHES

EVA WAS COOKING IN the enormous palace kitchen and enjoying small talk with her two guys. Senias, her new dragon friend, and Devon, her new mate. They had truly been having a great time at it. Both men taste testing everything and snacking on some fresh bread the cooks had left for them. Then, they all got interrupted by a slamming door and a pissy-looking Gareth walking through to find something in the cooling cupboard.

~ Bet she told him, ~ Senias mentally whispered to Devon. He waited. He was never sure what the hell was about to happen with the little brother. Gareth was quite the wildcard sometimes. But then, his dragon mate liked her barbaric types...

~ Oh yeah, she told him and he ain't none too pleased about it either. ~ Devon raised both of his shaggy brows at the dragon while taking a drink.

"Is it true?" Derek's voice came from the same door Gar had busted through. The dirty blonde-haired lycan stood near as tall and broad as his mentor sitting at the table. That Derek and Gareth were best friends and were physical opposites was funny. But nothing was funny about Derek's expressions. His bright eyes were full of questions as he looked at Senias. Then, as if he'd just noticed that Gareth was still searching the kitchen, he yelled, "Top shelf past the stove. Whiskey's behind the vase."

"That..." Senias was about to say that was *his* whiskey when Devon shook his head. The dragon conceded with a huff.

Pulling the whiskey down, Gareth didn't even bother with mugs. He opened it and took a good drink before answering his friend, "Of course it's true. She wouldn't have said anything if they didn't mean to leave." Gareth took another drink before offering the bottle to Derek.

Derek took the whiskey easily enough. He looked over at Senias. The draconic man took a deep breath and exhaled with a depressed sigh.

Everything was quiet, drinks and glares were shared. Then, the dragoness herself walked through the door; her eyes fixed on her lover. Inea with her long blonde waves and deep dark almost violet-blue eyes and golden tan stood almost regal in her calm confidence.

Gareth pushed his fingers through his messy black mane on the unbraided side. He glared in frustration at her with his pale crystalline blue eyes, barely able to restrain the tempest inside of him.

Inea paused; her fingers coming together in front of her. The depth of the emotion in the dragon's eyes was painful. She moved around the table toward Senias instead of taking her normal route to Gareth.

Eva watched, taking it all in. Senias couldn't blame her. She was still learning. The way she handled herself spoke of an excellent choice for Alpha.

Gareth looked at Inea's dragon mate as he licked his lips and handed the bottle off again. "So, Sen, when are ya headin' back?"

"I'm not sure. I've not talked to your father and mother about it..."

"Inea says less than a week. Is it the same for you?"

"I'm staying for Eva and Devon's ceremony. I wouldn't miss it." Senias looked from Gareth to Devon. His hand moved up Inea's back when she sat next to him, offering support through touch. "But I feel the same as Inea feels - that it's time we made our way back to face what we had to leave. So, if you have trouble with her, you have trouble with me."

"But y'all came here cause that world was goin' bad." Gareth rumbled low.

"It is not the world that is at fault, Gareth. Our world is beautiful and appropriate for us. We had to leave because of the dominating species, because Crimsons marked us, and because hunters were having their way with us. But we have connections there and responsibilities. I've bought arrangements that can see us through - aliases. Crimson cannot tell we are draconic unless we fuck up. They've stopped the active search. We can go back."

"It was always in our plans to return to our home world. We've remained here because your pack showed us kindness. We both wanted to ensure that you had peace before we left."

"But you've become our friends and... more." Derek's glances indicated he was obviously referring to Gareth.

"It will be once we push the elves back beyond the Northern Mountains," Kieran said as he walked into the room. Seeing Eva, the Alpha smiled. "Well now, I was told there would be good Gaian food coming from the kitchen. Sounds like the little bird what whispered that to me was correct, aye?" The Alpha's gaze caught sight of Gareth and Derek, and the whiskey halfway between the two. He growled. "What's this about?"

"Ask the dragons. They don't want ta be here anymore." Derek took a quick - possibly last - drink of the whiskey.

"You shouldn't go after the elves," Senias stated.

"They've lost their military leadership. They're on the run and took out a whole pack just for spite! And you want me to back down?" Kieran turned slowly to the dragon.

"You had dragons. Next time, you won't. We're going back across the portals to Gaia." Senias remained seated, but his eyes had no issue meeting Kieran's gaze. "Let your family enjoy some respite from war. Your entire pack is sick of it."

"You're abandoning the cause when we could finally finish it all off?" Kieran's chest growled low.

"You've finished it Kieran. And you don't want us to be here for another fight."

"Yes. Yes, I DO want you here! You're my partner in this conquest, Sen! You may not have started it, but you joined us, and you've become part of these warriors! Both of you helped free our people. You can't just leave!"

"This wasn't supposed to be a conquest, Kieran!" Senias stood up. "This was supposed to be a liberation! And it is done. I can leave and I will." Senias motioned for Inea to move back to the door behind Devon, for the Alpha had a nasty temper. The dragoness didn't waste a moment. The move was a good call.

One of Kieran's hands grabbed the vacated chair the dragon had been using, and it became a pile of rubble once it hit the far wall. Everyone in the room was on the move after that! This was a tight spot for a brawl, despite the rooms being made for a lycan.

Devon quickly stood in front of Eva.

Senias did not flinch. Kieran came right up to him, a hot breath in his face. The lycan was much broader and at least a foot taller. The two stared at each other, growling.

Stepping from behind Devon, Eva whistled as loudly as she could to get everyone's attention. And she got it.

"Now - in case you don't know it - those two dragons are hurting just as deep and sometimes deeper than anyone else in this room! I can see it in their auras. If I was in their shoes... I would make sure parting ways went as smoothly as possible. So, I'd ignore and hide my own emotions. That doesn't mean the emotions aren't there." Eva took a breath, smoothed her hands down her apron, and cleared her throat.

Everyone was looking at the newcomer... and while she had their attention, she continued her speech.

"Now you people can act a fool and be horrible to each other or you can be proper and enjoy the time you have left to spend together. I know if it were me, I'd make the most of the time given. And I'd not cause a mess of the kitchen where someone was tryin' not to burn her perfect meal. Especially since it's a meal she planned on sharing with everyone here." She huffed and stamped her foot on the floor, her chin raised.

Kieran turned around and moved out of the door he had come in through. Senias watched the big Alpha but didn't move immediately. Inea came to his side and touched his shoulder and then moved her fingers and palm over his upper back. She was doing her best to calm her mate, just as he had helped her. She said something draconic, something only a few lycan understood.

"What'd she say?" Derek whispered as quietly as he could to Gareth, for he hadn't a clue, and he knew his friend had spent much more time with the dragons than he did.

"She's tryin' to calm him and saying that leaving is the right thing to do. They are dangerous." Gareth shoved the half-empty bottle into his friend's hands. He hadn't been quiet in the sharing. Then, he spoke pointedly at Inea. "You left out the part where ya have a kindred over there that ya miss and that we don't mean a thing compared to that." Gareth left the room not long behind his father.

Inea's frown heralded her tears. Senias turned and took Inea in his arms and held her against his chest.

"Well, that prince doesn't think before he strikes, especially when he's being defensive. Makes me wonder why he's still a scout-in-training. Inea, you did what was right. We're doing what's right." Senias' gaze met Devon's as the elder prince settled back into his chair. The drama was finished for now.

"Food ready darlin'? I'm a starving man." Devon smiled for his future mate.

"Yes, I suppose you all can at least have a good lot of it." She piled his plate high with the beans and rice and sweet-hot venison they had brought back and tenderized mercilessly. Then she made her own plate, not near as much food on it. "Everyone come and get something to eat. Then, maybe it'll be time to look at the stars for a while? Let your energy get back to where it should be." She handed Devon his plate and took her own to join him wherever he sat.

"We'll be off for now. But thank you, Eva. The samples were delicious, and the offer was gracious." When he wanted to be, Senias could be gentle and kind. Right now, Inea needed that from him.

"Seems like everybody's hurting and starving themselves silly." Derek sighed and grabbed a plate to fill up. As he sat down, he motioned toward the dragons with his bread. "I'm gonna miss y'all ta be sure. You're my friends." The young warrior sopped up the juices on his plate with the bread and took a nice big bite.

"We'll miss you, too, ya big furball." Senias smirked. He put his hand around Inea's shoulders and led her out the door. As they left, he could hear Derek say something he could completely and totally understand.

"All this heartache? That's why I don't get serious with nobody."

Chapter Sixteen

The Mating Ceremony

The drums were beating, and the two moons were full above them. Helena smiled at the young woman that was being prepared for her union. "Look Evalyn, The Goddess is blessing your mating. You have two full moons for it."

"I see." Eva's voice was a little higher than usual. She had images of tripping up the stairs to the dais and landing on her ass. Forgetting what to do? Saying the wrong thing? Oh, so much...

"Five other Packs have come to this celebration to witness your union. Do you have questions before I leave you to start the celebration with Kieran?" Helena gave Evalyn one more look to make sure that she was perfect. The girl was breathtaking.

Evalyn had been taking lessons and soaking things up over the time she had to prepare for this. She had asked questions and had even taken to keeping notes that the shaman had suggested for prayers, blessings, and ceremonies. Helena had insisted that Evalyn spend a good portion of her day with both shamans to gain their wisdom and start an apprenticeship with them. And through it all, she had been patiently waiting for this night and this moment.

"No. But I'm still all nerves, I'm afraid." Eva was honest. Knowing how many eyes would look upon her only helped to make the nerves worse. There were already rumors about her spreading through the pack women - little on other packs.

The Alphas of other packs wanted to be connected to Pack Weylyn. They were the richest, most fruitful, and most powerful of all the lycan packs in this realm. Being connected to them meant safety and wealth for the future. And she was taking one of their sons - the one who was to be the heir. She...who had nothing to give so far as these other packs were concerned?

"You'll be fine Evalyn." Reaching for the bowl with the gold paint in it, Helena dipped her entire palm in it and started a new tradition. She pressed her palm over the curve of Evalyn's breast above her heart and spoke softly, "I bless you, daughter, with a golden future mated to my son. You'll be a great shaman and a powerful partner for him. You'll guide not only this Pack but help Devon know what's right. There are many beautiful children in your future, and some will no doubt give you heartache. Learn from it and never give up."

Eva nodded, and a bit of a smile spread over her lips. Leaning in so her daughter Alexis and the servant couldn't hear her, Helena added one final bit that was meant for Evalyn's ears alone.

"Remember, Eva, that together you are strong, nurturing, understanding, determined, and can overcome anything. Your love will teach others to love, and many will look to you and Devon as an example. If you turn from him or part with him, it will only bring misery. Love, faith, loyalty, and strength. I see all of it in you both. Never lose sight of that or you'll lose one another. I have told him the same." As she stepped back and peeled her hand away to leave the golden palm print in place, the Alpha smiled. "That is my blessing for you and your union, Evalyn."

"Thank you, Lady Helena," Eva quickly wiped unshed tears from her eyes. At least she knew she had the approval of the family and the shaman of this pack. She had proven herself capable and strong, resourceful and skilled. The others might not know, but she had something to give them all. She had even gotten the approval of some of the other ladies in the pack that would have been her rivals more recently. Some she would consider friends in the future, she was sure.

And Lady Helena was correct. She was everything Devon needed. He had proven that he was everything she needed. It was as if the Goddess had made her go through so much and when she thought there wasn't much more left; the Goddess gave her this gift as an apology. This new chance...

As the rhythm of the drums changed, Alexis, Devon and Gareth's little sister, finished Evalyn's markings. She drew golden sigils on the parts of Eva's body that were exposed for all to see, her mid-drift, her shoulders, part of her back, and her legs. Alexis seemed to enjoy having a sister and had done the best job she could do. Putting the paint down, she beckoned Eva, "Come listen, the celebration is beginning, my parents will start things. You can watch the announcements."

Before the eyes of all gathered, Helena held Kieran's hand and smiled for their people. The big Alpha read the announcements of deaths, births, expected births, and new courtings. To one side the dragons she had met stood together. To the other, Argoth and his mate, Leia, stood. Both had intricate tattoos on their hands that marked their original pack. Derek and Gareth were together near Devon.

Kieran read out the upcoming matings, which included their daughter and Devon's sister, Alexis, to Ethan of Simoa. There were moments of silence for those that had gone to the fields and rounds of cheers with howls for the rest. It was a very joyful celebration. The last announcement was for the mating of their son.

"Just keep your eyes on Dev and it will go smoothly, I promise." Alexis pointed out her brother as he moved from behind the dais to stand beside his father.

Eva didn't need anyone to point Devon out. She could feel him already. He was steady and strong - the matching foundation for their future together. He was the only creature she had ever had such an affinity for.

He wore nothing more than the breechcloth, which was traditional for the men in such ceremonies. Like Eva, they had covered Devon's body in sigils and symbols in gold that stood out on his skin. There wasn't an inch of fat on him, and he was tall and broad-built like his father. He had his mother's smile and loving demeanor. Devon was the best of both parents. The only other items on him were his beaded braids and a bicep cuff of polished silver. The cuff had the Pack emblem of a snarling wolf with a crown and three claw marks through it all.

The moment the drums stopped, Alexis opened the curtain and nodded to Evalyn, so she'd go. Pressing a kiss on her cheek, Alexis stepped back to give the lady time to shine. Head tipped high, Eva took the skirting in front of her to tuck partially in the waistband, and then she made her way to the opening of the tent.

Devon focused his amber gaze on the tent at the back of the crowd. People gasped at the sight of Eva. She wore a white and cream-colored skirts split up the sides and splattered with gemstones of all colors. The top piece hugged her breasts and bared her midriff. The colors highlighted her darker skin tone, and a silver clasp held her tight red curls.

His breath caught. She was gorgeous, and as she started her way along the path through the crowd, Devon had to hold himself back. This was her walk to make and if he interfered, he'd be saying she wasn't strong enough to stand up for her claim as his mate.

Several female lycan stepped into her path to growl and challenge her claim on Devon. He had warned her of such. Eva only needed to hold her head high and move past them. It was a show of strength.

Eva knew where she belonged. She made her way to the steps, giving two women little smirks. The ex-slave had won them over as allies already. They had come forward just for the fun and sport of it. Otherwise, she moved and responded with the grace and poise of the queen she already knew herself to be.

When she neared the dais, Devon moved down the steps and closed the last few feet to take his mate's hands with a grin that was full of pride for her. "I told ya, I had faith in ya and that you'd make it. Now here we are, are ya ready darlin'?"

"Yes, time to be officially yours in the eyes of everyone here, not just for the Goddess."

Devon was speechless and just caught in the moment right then. Where he had once seen uncertainty and hesitance in Eva, he now saw determination and desire. As they held each other's gazes, it was as if the rest of the world ceased to exist.

Kieran cleared his throat. "You gonna keep us waiting, son?" he asked with a chuckle. His smiling eyes moved to his mate at that moment. There was a shared smirk between them.

"Sorry." There was a blink of his golden eyes and Devon flushed before walking Eva up the rest of the way to the center of the dais.

Eva continued to hold one of Devon's hands as they took their places. She stopped repeating the words in her head and instead focused on what he was doing and saying. That was what everyone had told her to do. And so, yes... she would do it. She wanted to remember everything properly to say and do, but if it meant missing something beautiful that her mate said to her, then... was it worth all that? No. Devon rumbled softly for Eva as they faced one another a moment before speaking.

"The wars I fought and the peace that was so hard won? It was for moments like this. I searched packs and celebrations for years, hoping to feel a spark of something with every woman I crossed paths with." There were chuckles that spread through the crowd. "I hadn't really thought there was that perfect mate out there for me and I resigned my fate to an arranged mating. Then I saw the most glorious sight of my life when I saw ya dancing beneath the light of the half-moons. No other would do after that. I'd seen the woman that would hold my heart and my soul within her for the rest of our lives." He waited, letting Eva speak.

"I had so much taken from me; I became stronger than most. I learned not to trust anything or anyone. Sometimes, I didn't even trust myself. I wasn't looking for a mate and told myself I didn't need one. I was just looking for peace and a reason to keep going. Maybe I hoped to understand who I could never be. When I met you, my soul told me you were special. But I didn't trust myself, remember?" She smiled at him. "So, it took you a bit. But when you showed me I could trust myself, no matter what the outcome? That's when I knew being with you is what I DO need. I wasn't looking for you, but the Goddess brought you to me, anyway."

Kieran moved toward the couple, ready to make everything official.

"As Alpha of Pack Weylyn, I, Kieran, join these two souls." He placed the embroidered cloth that Helena had provided over their joined hands. Then, he wrapped first one side and then the other further up their wrists. "Devon, speak your oath, from the heart."

"As we stand beneath the light of the Goddess' full moons, I pledge myself to you, Evalyn La Croix. I will always keep you safe and warm and always provide all that you and our future pups may need to be healthy and well. I will hold and comfort you all the days of our lives. I will listen to your wisdom and accept your guidance. Within our household, we are equal and any that stand before one will face both. I love you with all that I am and all that I ever will be. My heart beats with yours and you are my soul. The day that you take your last breath, I will go to the fields with you. This is my oath and my eternal pledge to you, Eva."

His mother was wide-eyed but held her tongue. The pledge he made was more than a simple one to take Evalyn as his mate. He'd never take another mate. There would be no severing this bond if Evalyn accepted it.

A tear fell from Eva's eye and ran down her cheek. Her lips trembled. She closed her eyes and swallowed to find her voice again. For a moment, people around them seemed worried.

"As we stand beneath the light of our Goddess," she began, then cleared her throat. She found his beautiful eyes and felt his strength boost her own. "I pledge myself to you, Devon Weylyn. I will comfort you when you need it, and always give you a safe place away from all that seeks to hurt or haunt you. I will happily raise pups with you and grand pups." Eva gave him an impish grin. "I will hold you and defend you and our family fiercely all the days of our lives. I will listen and give you guidance while also taking yours to heart. For we will be equals in all that we do, all that we plan, and all that we face. When you take your last breath, I will go to the fields with you. And that is my oath and my eternal pledge to you, Devon." She squeezed his hand beneath the kerchief and her eyes did not leave his. She meant it.

His father finished securing the cloth and Devon didn't wait for any closing remarks as he drew Eva to him and kissed her deeply. His free arm wrapped around her waist to draw Eva up on her tiptoes as the kiss continued to the whoops and yells of encouragement from their audience. They would dance a bit, eat a little, and then? Well then, Devon would steal his mate away to vanish for over a week into the place he'd set up for them. Eva couldn't wait. But first, there was the celebration going on all around them.

She could hear the rest of the pack's up-and-comers getting ready for the hunt. And then the rest of the adults were dancing or eating and drinking. Some were probably just visiting and enjoying themselves. Someday, she and Devon would be in charge of all of this. It boggled the mind.

Nipping at the shell of his new mate's ear, Devon growled low, "Want me to hunt you? We can join in if ya like?"

"No. You've already hunted me, and you'll hunt me down again. Tonight, I want you to take me, mark me, make me yours... and I'll make you mine. Then, I just want to have you and enjoy you to myself without the rules and the nerves and the pushing and the talking. Please?"

"For you, anything," Devon growled softly for Eva and moved with her through the next round of dancing. They lasted for two dances, and then Devon slipped away with her. Loosening the material on their arms so they could hold hands better, they ran from the celebration. Out past the stream, Devon unwound the sash and placed it around Eva's neck. They slipped through the wooded area and up into the hills. Devon stopped before a small cabin. He was grinning with pride.

"I built this with my older brothers before they went off to the first wars. I brought food, drink, and blankets up for us to use." Devon looked Eva up and down as if he were deciding on where to begin. Eva, on the other hand, had no trouble with where to begin.

Chapter Seventeen

WISHFUL THINKING

SENIAS WAS STANDING NEXT to Inea at the edge of the dais. They were both enjoying the ceremony and its grandeur. They had dressed in splendid creams and tans and mochas, lovely cotton, linen, and silk clothing that matched well. Inea had a silver and crystal crown that sat upon her brow over her flaxen hair, a single pearl hanging to her forehead. Senias wore a chain at his neck with an amethyst crystal set in the center of rubies and blackened metal. It was only the size of a thumb, but it was eye-catching on his nearly bare chest - a gift from one he hoped to find again.

The dragons hoped to share this moment with the new couple, supporting their friends in a celebration blessing the pack. Hopefully, Devon and Eva's children would never know about war. The dragons planned on this last night, perhaps sharing a drink or two, then they would be gone on the morrow. This was not their place anymore. They stayed until everything was right with the pack.

Inea turned her head to the side, feeling the gaze of her lover who stood closer to his royal family.

~ If this is to be our last evening, could we not just forget the rest of the world and everything to come and enjoy one another? ~

Gareth was still angry, of that there was no doubt. Yet when she called out to him, his bright blue gaze sought hers where she stood at Sen's side.

Once the new couple was off, Gareth slipped from the dais. Moving through the crowd to reach Inea, he stopped before her. After trading silent looks with Senias, he took the dragoness by the hand and vanished with her. If this was to be their last evening together, he wanted to make sure it was one that she wouldn't soon forget.

"Don't kill him." Senias shook his head as the two sped off together. Inea's laughter echoed through the growing crowd.

"Dancing first?" Inea asked as she turned to put her arms around Gareth's shoulders.

"Sure Flutters, anything ya want." Gareth smiled at her, and it lit up his bright blue eyes. He moved with her, and she laughed as he spun her around.

"Oh! Very well then." She loved the mixture of her world's dancing and his world's dancing that they often did. It was a change, and he kept her on her toes. She reacted perfectly and ended up back in his arms, giggling. It also warmed her to hear her nickname being used.

"See, I can still make ya smile and laugh and enjoy yerself." His canines showed as he grinned at her before drawing her close to nuzzle and breathe her scent in.

As they danced, they could see all the others enjoying the fun. Derek had his little sister Twilight dancing with him while their mother and father had a dance. Even his parents, as much as they did things separately, were dancing to this first set of music. He felt like a lot of eyes could be on them.

"Feel like runnin' with me? We could have our hunt away from the others." His brows danced up and down as his grin turned wicked for Inea.

"I'd love that." She stepped away but grasped his hand in her own. They took off running out to the side of the woods where the newly mated couple had a cabin. The official hunt would be on the opposite side of the forest. They knew to avoid the cabin, and as they got farther into the wilds, Inea turned to wait on Gareth to shift. Her dragon form was too large for this place, or she'd join him. The moment they were far enough off from the gathering, Gareth shifted and let Inea climb onto his back. He took off running, weaving through trees, and going over hills. He just enjoyed both the closeness and the thrill of the run with his dragoness!

At least they were enjoying it until he raced through a gathering of trees, jumped a large deadfall, and landed right in the center of a group of ... elves?

"Elves!" ~ What are they doing here? Wait... did we go the wrong way? ~ Gareth had slid to a halt and quickly shifted direction to rush past the tents that were set up just like the lycan tents would be. He even smelled lycan all around them, not elves. So how had they done this? He went to make a go of escaping, but he found the way quickly cut off by yet another group of elves... or were they lycan? He was so confused!

Inea held on for dear life! The forest was so thick here, she couldn't imagine shifting to her dragon form without possibly fatal damage. Every angle that Gareth took led to more enemies.

~ This ain't good! Can ya get away to let pops and the others know? ~

~ I'm not leaving you! Get far enough and I can cast a portal in front of you! ~ Inea held on tighter with her knees and raised her hand palm-out and focused on the space several yards in front of them. Suddenly, something slammed into her face, sending her bowling backward off Gareth's back.

Gareth hit the trip wire at full force and as Inea went flying off him one way, the big black wolf went tumbling in the other. ~ Nea! ~

Inea groaned as she slowly raised herself off the pine-needle carpet. She had blood running from her brow and nose. What was worse? She was feeling around as if she couldn't see. The air was smoky around her. Breathing it in made the woman cough and then wretch.

Whoever had set the trap up was smart because before Gareth could go into his hybrid form, a spell slammed into his chest. He reverted his body to the human form. He was coughing and trying to crawl to his dragoness.

"That's it, beautiful serpent. Breathe it in." The words made Gareth growl, and he tried once again to shift to his deadly form. Alas, he felt something else hit him from behind. The elves and lycan surrounding him quickly bound him and gathered him up for transport.

"Nay...sol...solumn..." Inea collapsed again to the ground, struggling to breathe.

"Was she trying to speak elvish?" An elf asked another. He kicked the woman in the gut as hard as he could manage and spat in her face. "She is nothing to this situation. Let us go."

ONLY A FEW HILLS away, Devon and Eva were finally alone and mated. There was no hesitation. They were mates in the eyes of the pack, and the Goddess gave her blessing by sprinkling her full moon fever upon them. Eva's hands moved to the ties in the side of his loincloth while she kissed him, their paints now smearing on their bodies.

Goddess above knew how badly he wanted to claim Eva as his mate, but Devon had learned long ago that good things come to those who wait. So, he was being patient. His golden gaze was drinking her in, but then that tingle of warning raced up his spine and sent every nerve he had flaring.

He went from adoring and eager to alert warrior in but a moment's notice. The way his stance changed to more of one that was ready to protect his mate. His change to his hybrid form placing her behind him nearer the cabin let Eva know they were not alone. Slowly, Devon drew in the air. His gaze narrowed as he growled.

Cloaked figures poised around them at the tree line. They were casting spells. Eva recognized the magic.

"No!" Eva tried to tug Devon back, but it was too late! Devon snarled, growled, and took one step forward before he fell like a massive tree to land with a powerful thud on the ground.

Eva growled, but before she let her inner wolf out, she heard a familiar voice.

"No, no, now girlie! It's done. No need ta ruin yer pretty self more. Fight and you'll just be doing yerself harm and we'll treat him worse." Madron Regis' voice called out.

"You…" Eva couldn't believe it! "The Alpha said it was a fair deal! Why have you done this?" She put herself over Devon, trying to keep them from her mate.

"The Alpha made a fair deal for you, then had my caravan raided by local authorities and Crimson. Slaves aren't the only things I trade. I lost a year's profit. So, he still owes me. And I'm takin' back what's mine and then some."

When he made the mistake of putting his hands on her, Eva turned around, her hybrid form standing before them all. She went for the throat, but he blocked her with his arm. She was in a fury and took it, slinging her head from side to side. Regis went flying, his flesh ripping and his cries full of pain. If they didn't do something, Madron Regis would lose more than his years' worth of profit. Lucky for the slaver, the Elven spells hit Eva as they had Devon. She let go, stumbled backward, and landed on top of her mate, both in their weaker human forms.

"Well..." Regis swallowed and grunted in pain as he held his now useless arm. "She's already learned a thing or two. Might not even be worth it ta sell her again."

"Don't..." Eva whispered. Her mixed blood was her blessing. She could still hear them and though things were whirling in her mind, she swore she recognized a voice - not just the old slaver's voice, but a feminine one. She tried to keep focus.

"Wrap his wounds and stop the blood flow. We do not need a trail available to be followed. Madron Regis, the prisoners are yours along with the others in that cart."

"What am I ta do with them, eh?" Regis asked.

"I don't care what you do with them, so long as they're gone for good."

Eva watched the tattooed hand as it passed close to her face. Then she felt two fingers on the pulse point in her neck.

"Once Kieran Weylyn has lost his pups, and the Eleven leader takes his revenge, retribution will be complete. A new pack can take over as the lead pack. A pack that will be honorable. A pack that will not continue to take our lives."

CHAPTER EIGHTEEN

OTHER PEOPLE'S DRAMA

SENIAS WALKED AWAY FROM all the dancing and merriment that was to be had around the huge bonfire. The draconic man preferred to be alone inside the keep. He had his own bottle of spirits and a quiet kitchen. He wasn't sure how long he had sat there, drinking and letting his mind wander over his memories when someone interrupted.

"What's yer problem, claw?" Kieran asked as he flopped down at the kitchen table, far away from the whoops and hollers of the dance outside the keep's walls.

"I could ask the same of you?" Senias was leaning his head on one hand while playing with the cup of whiskey in the other. "Don't you have a mate to dance with?"

"Don't you?" Kieran put it back to him.

"You know that's not how we work. She's off diddling yer son. You know she loves that idiot, right?" Senias looked over the cup before he finally took it and downed it in a single swallow. "She's not in her needing time, so I've no interest in her delicacies. Only her friendship."

"Your kind work in very mysterious ways, Sen." Kieran picked up the half-full bottle and clicked his tongue against his teeth.

"For a lycan understanding, I suppose so." Senias watched Kieran pour another. Here they were, not long past the night that Kieran had stormed out after smashing his chair against a wall - drinking with one another. That was just how most lycan were. "Something wrong with Helena?"

"She's not feeling it proper. Danced the opener and then she needed to excuse herself. The Goddess blessed me with a mate that has her own issues during the full moons." Kieran got up to grab himself a cup. He came back to the table and poured another drink. He put the bottle down and picked the cup up to stare at the brandy fluid for a moment before taking a drink, then hissing a bit with the burn.

"That's not how ye drink whiskey," Senias slurred.

"It's how I want ta. So, hush." The Alpha chuckled as he scolded his friend. "When we were out in the field, you had secret lovers to your bed. You afraid people would get pissy with ya if you danced with one of them tonight?" He was curious.

"I don't care what they think about me. I care what someone will face once I leave. They must live on in this pack and male being with male, your culture doesn't accept it. It's something I see as wrong among your pack laws." Senias took a deep breath. "But it's the same elsewhere. In our lands, it's not a practical thing. Here it's about procreation. And I get that, I just don't get that once a man procreates and cares for a woman who wants to procreate... he and she can't just enjoy others who are like-minded. We dragons have been doing so for generations. Inea likes men and so do I."

"What do they say about it over there?" Kieran asked.

"They say it's a sin."

"A Sen...?" Kieran was confused and amused.

"No, it's ... although that's funny," Senias chuckled. "It's their dominating religious belief. Most of them see anything that's not for procreation as a sin - a word for something evil. They have a deep lack of pleasure from what I've seen. Doesn't mean sexual pleasure's wiped out, but it's not something so open as you have here. But that's what confuses me about here - how people get treated for laying with their own when ye..you are so open otherwise." Sen sighed and took down the next cup.

"Maybe we should work on that." Kieran wasn't above thinking over the pack's philosophies. "It might take a while, but knowing you and those that frequented your tents over the years? That puts the whole situation in a better perspective. I trust all of you with my life out there in the war zones. Just because you like to fuck each other instead of women don't matter to battle or loyalty. Maybe, if I come up with new ways around the procreation situation? Or... the mating situation..."

"So, that'd be my reason for staying out of the dance. My mind is on one person in particular, anyway. And I don't even know if he's yet alive..."

There was a noise from the backside of the kitchen door, near the trellis and shed.

"What was..." Senias was sitting up straight in an instant. He could go from drunk to sober in a few minutes, given the need.

With her golden hair spilling down from its usual tight knot, and a flush to her cheeks that made her appear much younger than she was, Helena stepped into the kitchen. She paused at the sight of the two men sharing the bottle. As she felt Kieran's gaze move over her, assessing her, she was quickly trying to snatch her hair back. Senias thought perhaps she was trying to seem less appealing to her mate.

"Good evening Senias, I hear you'll be departing to return to the other world and that Inea is going with you." The dragon noted that the woman was actively trying not to look at Kieran.

"Why did you..." Senias' brows pulled down and he held a finger up. He looked from the normal two entryways that led from the courtyard inside and one from the inner sanctum. Then he looked back to Helena and the way she had come in from the outside where the kitchen patio was. His half-drunken mind was trying to piece things together.

"Senias, I would appreciate it if you gave me a moment with my mate." Kieran's golden eyes didn't leave Helena. Helena's gaze remained on Kieran right then. Her chin went up just a touch.

Sen watched both of them. He seemed nervous about it. But he picked up the whiskey and a glass. He looked at Helena. ~ You are sure, m'lady? ~

"Senias, if you mind-talk to her one more time, I'm aiming ta knock ya through that wall inta next week. Wanna try me, considering how drunk ya are?" Kieran's eyes were hard like cobalt. But he added, "I don't aim ta hurt my mate. But I need ta talk to her alone."

"It's all right Senias, go enjoy the rest of the evening. I'll be okay." Helena gave the dragon a warm smile of appreciation and nodded to him.

"Fine." Senias walked to the side and closed first one door and then went out the other.

As the door closed, leaving them alone, Helena clasped her hands before her but made no moves from her current place. She would not join him at the table, nor was she bolting from him.

"And what are we to talk about, Kieran?"

"You can't even be discreet about it anymore?" He asked a low growl in the back of his throat. That told her how upset he was at that moment.

"As discreet as you and your women? It's a miracle you don't have dozens of bastards within this very Pack."

"I only started takin' lovers because my mate wouldn't have me!" Kieran growled, then his eyes grew fierce. He turned away from her and rested his palms on the big metal table.

Helena rubbed her forehead with two fingertips. "Kieran, what is it you want or expect from me? Do I not stand at your side and smile when you need me to? Have I not been an exemplary mother to our children?"

"Have I not shown you love from the moment we were told to court? Have I not given you everything I can give you? Can you not love me anymore?" He turned and looked at her. "Didn't we have some good times? All our children weren't born out of obligation, were they? Or were they?" He wanted to hear her say something about this. He'd questioned this over and over and over again.

"I told you when you asked my father for my hand that I loved another. We were to be mates. That never changed. You had my father in dire straits, and you knew it. He demanded I be mated to you to join our packs. I don't want to hurt you, but no, I don't love you. I love our children. You wanted heirs, and I gave you heirs." Tears sparkled at the corners of her eyes. "Three of them have stones beneath the Great Oak because they followed you to war."

"That wasn't my choice..." Kieran whispered.

"Let me go and we'll leave. He wants to." Helena pleaded with her mate.

"If I let ya go right now, your pack would be shamed, and I would be shamed and you'd have nothing but him. He no longer has a pack, Helena. Argoth may have been a prince at one time, but the elves scattered his pack to the winds. You know this. The only reason he and his family yet live is that they are travelers. They have taken our pack's name. You are not a traveler. You ain't used ta anything but courtly life. If it came out that you'd both betrayed me, the elders would kick all the ones that we took in off our lands. They'd have nothing. Nor would you. It's not a threat - it's just the truth."

Helena swallowed and her gaze dropped away from him, "Not true. I would have my children."

"No. I won't let you take my pups. Not when they have a life here. This is all they've known, Hel. That wouldn't be right." He took a deep breath and walked toward the door to the back patio, past her.

"Then we remain at an impasse because I won't leave my children." She drew in a breath, "I will remain discreet, Kieran, I just ask that you do the same."

"Then I guess I'll join up with the druids of the forests. They're celibate. Cause I can't exactly hide who I am." He kept walking. And then he was shifting. And then he was running. Because that's what you did when you had no one to help you with a secret you couldn't share.

CHAPTER NINETEEN

A DRAGON'S GLARE

HELENA LET HER BREATH out in a big burst. She hadn't realized she had been holding it. She put a hand on the table near her, bending a bit and holding her diaphragm as she took in several gulps of air.

"Sooo... he's wrong about the druids. They're not exactly celibate." Senias' voice came from the next room.

The woman's eyes became enormous as she made her way through the kitchen to the door on the other side and around the wall to see the dragon sitting there. He was pouring the last of the whiskey into the cup. Then he looked at the lovely woman who rounded the wall, toasted her, and downed the drink.

"Oh, blessed Goddess, have you been there the whole time?" Slowly Helena sat down in the chair across from the dragon, groaning as she did.

"You know... I'm not unsympathetic, Helena." The dragon whispered his words, being as soothing as he could. "I just usually hate drama. Find myself in the middle of it all the time. But hate it."

"I just..." She covered her face with both hands as tears rolled down her cheeks, "He refuses to let me go even as he knows I don't love him. Or I could leave, but I'd go without my children. And if the truth came out - all Argoth's pack would pay, too. I've already sent three sons to the fields. I can't lose my others. We're trapped. And I'm growing to hate Kieran for my cage."

"Kieran's stuck in the cage with you, or haven't you noticed?" Senias pointed out. "It's apparently a cage of his own making, or perhaps his parents' making. We were just talking about how traditions need to be changed. Traditions can be a cage." The dragon pulled his feet up into the big chair with the rest of his body and watched her.

"It's a cage of his choosing." Her voice held a snarling edge to it. "You heard him, Senias. If I leave him, then the pack will shun all of us. I will lose my children. So my only choice is to remain and keep this quiet as we have while Kieran makes a fool of me..."

"You know, had anyone seen you come in that door but us, you'd be making a fool of him. It was obvious where you came from and what you'd been doing. And it had nothing to do with being sick, so your lie is obvious."

Helena huffed angrily, but she slowly nodded, conceding his opinion.

"Why did Argoth take a mate if ...I... I understand that lycan place a high value on their female mates, but they also sometimes force matings. So, what happened here? How did this mess begin?"

"When the lycan took their freedom from the elves, vampires, and dragons. We had packs, but no leaders outside of those packs. There was chaos and then slowly the packs realized there needed to be an Alpha Pack that could lead the others during times of war. The Alphas challenged each other, and Kieran came out the victor." Helena took a deep breath. "As the new Alpha of our kind, they gave Kieran his choice amongst each pack's eligible women. I was being courted by Argoth when he saw me." Wiping her face, Helena took in a shaky breath.

"He demanded my hand from my father, and to make the alliance of a lifetime, my father agreed." Golden eyes looked right at the dragon, "I told Kieran I loved another and he said time changed all things. If I denied him? My family's pack would suffer the rejection as would Argoth's because Kieran would've gone after him. So, I accepted him and tried to make it work. I turned my back on Argoth and had my children with Kieran. Then I lost my three eldest to the first wars. Soon after, they captured Devon. We thought he was dead too. Then Argoth brought him home two years later. I didn't have it in me to turn from him again, Senias."

The dragon moved to put his hand on her shoulder, comforting her. How had he not seen this in the 8 years he'd been here? Helena couldn't believe it. She supposed it was a testament to their ability to keep things discreet, despite what her mate had claimed. When the dragon sat back, she nodded a silent thanks and continued.

"He had tried to move on without me. The elves nearly wiped out his pack. Because he'd brought Kieran his son, he was a hero. Kieran offered what was left of Argoth's pack a place. He's Devon's best friend now, and he's a good man. I became pregnant with Gareth at the same time his mate was expecting Derek." Helena looked at her hands.

"Gareth..." Dark hair, crystalline eyes... eyes that looked a lot more like Argoth's eyes than Kieran's. "Fuck."

She licked her lips. "A few years later, there was a good time. I tried to make something with Kieran. Really, I did. I had Alexis while he was off finding war again after promising me he wouldn't. He'd promised not to take my son into it with him, but he did. I felt betrayed, Sen. I've been his mate in name only ever since."

Senias moved his fingertips along the top of the empty glass as he listened.

"I went back to Argoth, and Kieran started bedding the servants, enjoying himself in the camps and on the road. Argoth's mate had their baby girl, Twilight, to keep him away from me." She shook her head. "It didn't work."

"Neither of you has much control. Not that I blame you. I have quite a libido myself. My kindred and I knew it would be a long time and gave one another permission. I can't imagine betraying Sebastian." He was really trying to wrap his head around this. "It seems so damned hypocritical considering all the traditions surrounding monogamy at play with you lycan."

There was an elongated silence. They could hear the drums and instruments outside while they sat - two friends - studying one another.

"Let me handle Kieran," the dragon said suddenly. "And in the meantime, I have an offer for you." Senias took her hand in his and stood up. "Will you come with me?"

Helena nodded, and they walked down the stairs inside the west tower. He grabbed a small torch that he lit. At the end of the spiral staircase and then a small hallway, there was just a room with a lot of dust-covered cloths over furniture. Senias walked inside and turned to the wall beside the door. He placed his hand on an odd design made of inlaid brick from the stone wall. With but a small push, he had opened a secret door on the far side of the room.

When they stepped through, Helena was in the dark, but she still had Senias' hand. The draconic man spoke to her mentally. ~ Say the word Inata loudly, as if you were scolding someone. ~

"Inata!" Helena's voice took that sharp edge as she snapped the word out. She was, after all, the Alpha of this Pack and a mother, so she knew how to scold.

At the command, the torches all around the small lair lit up. In the center was a pad of gold, just big enough for the dragon to lie upon when he was in his true form. To one side was a stairway made of stone and brick. And where they stood, there was a chaise, two chairs, and a table all on top of a lovely large hand-woven rug. There was a warmth in the room that kept things comfortable despite it being underground.

"Oh..." The beautiful lycan looked around. "This is lovely Senias, but why bring me here?"

"I want you to have this. Everyone needs a place of their own. I never allowed Kieran to know where it was. I've only ever had Inea here with me. No one knows where to find it. But I'll leave my wards up for you." Senias took a deep breath. "I'll not be using it after tomorrow. Why let it go to waste? What has happened... you have no way out. But at least you have a place of privacy you can share with your true mate."

"Don't do that Senias. While I appreciate the offer, Kieran would find out and you'd lose his friendship." There was a sad smile on her face.

"Hmph... well... I'll deal with Kieran. Like I said. You just take care of yourself and the kids, and the pack. Devon's... Devon's one of my closest friends. And you're his mother. You deserve more respect than what you've gotten. I'm happy that you and Kieran had him, even if the circumstances are all focked up."

"Devon has always been different as fierce as his father or as gentle as I am while holding a babe. I'm very glad he has you as a close friend, Senias. Something tells me you'll only grow closer through the years. Even in absence, may that bond grow."

"I hope so." Senias took a deep breath as he admitted, "I only just realized how much I could trust Devon. I'm afraid I kept him at arm's length for the longest time. But he and Eva and I had some pleasant talks."

Helena stepped to the dragon and hugged him, "Thank you for listening to me and not thinking me too foul of a creature for my heart."

"Naaa..." Senias growled before taking her hand and leading her to the stairwell.

"I hope you find what you're returning through the portal for, but what will you do if the one you've gone back has passed on?"

"I don't know. I truly don't know." He tapped her arm and said, "Say the word again and the lights will go out here and they will go out once you pass them up the way."

"Inata!" There was a breathy little sigh with the word as she watched the lights go out in the lair.

"Well done." He was quiet as they ascended the stairs toward a distant light above. This was a different path leading out of the cave. Helena noted the locations of the doorways and the way to walk without stumbling. And then the dragon began speaking again. "If he has died, it will not be because of nature. Therefore, I will hunt down whoever caused his death." Senias touched her elbow to keep her moving.

Helena's heart ached for him. "I'll pray that's not the case. Perhaps he's tucked away pining for you?" Her smile was warm.

"Speaking of returning, I need to ask a favor of you."

"What is it you need, Senias? I'll do it if I can." The Alpha looked him right in the eyes.

"Devon's as stubborn as his father. So, I want to leave something in your hands." He took the necklace from around his neck, the one with the amethysts and rubies. "If any of them or if you need me... you can use this. It's powerful. You open it like a locket. Let the shard inside cut your hand so it has blood on it. Then close your eyes and call out to me. Not much will get to me, so don't go overboard, but... I will know that I'm needed. And I'll begin making my way back."

Studying the piece, she looked from it to Sen. "He gave it to you, didn't he? And you never used it? Why?"

"I was never in that much danger. Sebastian told me it was for emergency use. Missing him was not an emergency. I had to be strong and wait out the dangers we left behind."

"I'll keep it safe for you and hopefully I never have to use it and you get to return on your own for a friendly visit." Helena smiled at Senias.

"I'd like that." Sen turned to bow. Helena cocked her head, unsure what to think about the gesture. "It has been a pleasure serving you and your pack, m'lady. In case we don't speak again."

CHAPTER TWENTY

THE OTHER WOLF

AFTER LEAVING HELENA, ARGOTH had come to the spring to wash off and had just pulled on his fresh clothes when of all people Kieran had stumbled up the hill toward him. The Alpha of Pack Weylyn was drunk, and that never ended well.

"You fuckin' curr! You have a mate! Keep to her!" Kieran came up the slope to stand on the level ground that Argoth was on. His eyes were aglow with his power, ready to shift. "Stay away from Helena. I'm done, Argoth. I'm done."

While built leaner and shorter than Kieran was, Argoth was no novice fresh to fighting. He could carry his own. He'd brought a near-dead Devon home, after all. While he wouldn't start a fight with the snarling lycan that was coming toward him, Argoth wouldn't turn away like a coward. Slowly, the dark-haired lycan shook his head and Argoth's crystal blue eyes shimmered with power, too.

"I'll not give you what you want anymore. You tried to rip us apart, and it's not happening again. I can't stay away from her, and you know that. It'd be like cutting out my heart. We've tried that. It didn't work." Argoth tossed the bag with his clothes in it to the side and tugged off his clean shirt to toss over with them. It was just in time to get his balance before Kieran ran him down.

The Alpha not only had Argoth down, but he also then shifted and picked the scout up and threw him against the stone wall nearby. Kieran was a warrior, a heavyweight. Argoth was a scout, nothing lacking where that was concerned, but against Kieran in hand-to-hand, well, the Alpha had strength and weight on his side. Shaking his head, Argoth rolled quickly, keeping himself out of reach of the big man. All he could do was deliver kicks and punches where possible and outlast his opponent.

They went several rounds before Argoth heard flapping wings coming from the direction of the palace. Argoth wasn't sure what to think about it, and Kieran's confidence seemed boosted even more by the thought of having his dragon on his side. Kieran took several hits, but then connected, sending his rival flying.

Argoth was in a heap on the ground for a moment or two before he forced himself to his feet. There was no way he was just going to let the man beat him to death without fighting back. Shifting to his hybrid form, Argoth roared and went after the larger lycan. He wasn't a fool, though. He didn't go headfirst into Kieran. The wiry built lycan used his body to his advantage to duck and dodge the blows coming his way.

Claws dug in and raked around Kieran's ribs before Argoth rushed out of the way. The beat of the dragon's wings distracted him. He felt the big hand land on his shoulder and tugged him backward.

Kieran growled viciously as he lifted his opponent off the ground and slammed him back into it, hitting his side. He literally bounced up from the force and Kieran then hit the other man's face with a nasty right hook, sending him spinning away.

Spitting blood, the other lycan got back up, and the fight continued. Even as Senias landed nearby they were tumbling and hitting. Argoth was refusing to stay down, even though he knew he had a broken rib, and his eye was swelling shut. He took his stance and prepared for the next round. His canines bared as he figured he was facing off with not only Kieran but the damned dragon too! He'd go down fighting!

When Kieran roared at Argoth and went down on all fours, Senias knew what he had to do. His friend was no longer thinking clearly. He moved swifter than most thought the dragon could.

Kieran had to pull up, as there was suddenly a scaled beast four times the size of a large wagon between him and Argoth. As he did, his clawed feet kicked off the scaled wall. The dragon made an odd keening whine. Blood ran from beneath a few of the scales where the lycan had indeed gotten to the flesh.

Had Senias not interceded, the dragon was certain Argoth would have taken a killing blow.

The Alpha turned quickly, circling counterclockwise. The dragon followed suit but stopped with his tail still very near Argoth's position, shielding the mongrel.

"What is this? Why did you stop me?!" Kieran roared with the question.

"You arrrrre wrong Kieran!" The dragon's voice was clear though deep and grating when he spoke in this form. The snarled growl afterward was just the way they talked. He lowered himself in a stance of defense near a completely confused Argoth.

Kieran's anger had him howling and roaring in his rage. And as he did, Senias roared above him so that the sound did not carry. No one would come from the celebration to witness this. Argoth growled from the side. Apparently, he had mended enough to think he had a good chance. But the dragon had had enough.

Neither of the lycan would ever mistake the sound of the dragon's bellows engaging. The gurgling and the chemicals in the dragon's lower throat pouch ignited. The fiery breath was ready. Molten slobber lit the ground where Senias's mouth couldn't hold all of it.

~ Stand down! Both! Or feel the pain of fire. ~ The dragon turned his head slightly and blew flaming spit onto the tree nearby to make sure he had their attention off this damned fighting. ~ Do not make your tragedy worse than it already is! ~

Kieran shifted completely and stood, his mouth partially open, his questioning gaze on the dragon.

Forced into human form by the pain, Argoth stood there clutching his side and wheezing. He was warily watching this dragon, who had always been at Kieran's side. He had never seen them at such odds.

The dragon gulped the flames back and swallowed, knowing his body would extinguish them. When this was done, the magical flash occurred and allowed him to shift. He looked down at his chest, blood now staining his white shirt, before he looked back up at Kieran.

"It was enough to carry through the transition." Senias focused on Kieran. "You were going to kill him?" the dragon asked, concern on his face.

Kieran growled low. He looked away from the dragon.

"You were going to kill one of the most loyal men you have in your pack, your son's best friend, defender of all of your children, and true mate to your taken mate?" Senias stepped closer to Kieran as he laid it all out there for them. "How do you think all of them would respond to such an action? How do you think that would end?"

"You eavesdropping'..."

"I'm here to keep you from making the worst mistake of your entire life! Don't you dare try to pitch shit at me!" Sen's eyes glowed bright blue-green in his anger.

"I've already made the worst mistake of my life!" Kieran turned away from both and slammed his fist into a tree trunk. He put his head against the trunk and closed his eyes, fighting the dark emotions that rolled through him.

Senias turned quickly to Argoth. "Get your ass over here! Wounded or not. Welcome to the club. Both of you are going to listen to me since I don't think either of you has been listening to your mate."

Argoth turned back towards the two men and walked closer, though he remained out of Kieran's reach.

"She's not his mate," Kieran growled as he walked back over, hackles still up.

Senias put a finger up toward Argoth, "One moment, please." He turned to Kieran.

"Yes, she is. You are both her mates, and she cares about both of you, but let's be very clear - Argoth was her mate first, Kieran. And you need to accept tha—" Kieran could not have been more predictable considering he was an angry drunk. Senias would've rolled his eyes. Instead, he flipped and collapsed backward, letting Kieran's lunge pass over him. Then, he rolled and lifted his body up, using the strength of his arms to do so. Kieran turned and when he tried once again, this time Senias wound up on the Alpha's back and put him in a sleeper hold. "Stop now... or you know ...you'll wake up ...with me dumping... you in the water! Been here before, haven't we?" The dragon grunted.

Argoth stood back, impressed and obviously taking mental notes about that move.

It took a full minute before Kieran slapped the dragon's arm. Sen released him and watched him dive face-first into the ground near Argoth.

"I spoke to her, watched her, and listened to her. And I understand what she feels. I know what duty and responsibility feel like as it weighs heavily on your shoulders. I know what it feels like to have the expectations of many resting on your decisions. I know what it is to have the lives of so many in the balance. If she was selfish, she would ignore them all and go with her heart.

But your mate, she's not a selfish person. She took Kieran as a mate so that her pack would prosper. So that the young would have a better chance. And they have." He turned from Argoth to Kieran.

"Her heart belonged to Argoth before she made this decision. You knew it and you didn't stop the ceremony. That's on you. But she is now also your mate. Simple as that. You need to share. But I believe, old friend... you have fucked that chance. And you have taken advantage of certain situations to make things more difficult for her." He looked over at Argoth.

"I'm here to point things out to both of you before you hurt her or your children and other mate further. I'm here to sit with you for as long as it takes to get things worked out so that when I leave, there will be no more of this shit."

"Lycan don't share..."

"BULLSHIT!" Senias got up from the sitting position he was in and shook his head. He put his hands on Kieran's shoulder where the man sat. "I give you that is the case most of the time, but not all the time. Lycan can adapt. After all, you also told me lycan don't lie with their own sex. Would you like to know how many male lycan I've fucked?"

Kieran growled low.

"You acted like you were ready for changes earlier, in the kitchen. You know that many of your traditions are wrong. Your elders made them from a time when they were necessary. I'm here to tell you that if you do not change your ways, your pack will suffer. And the suffering will begin with you and your mate and your family." Senias backed up and took a deep breath into his lungs before letting it out slowly. "Therefore, like the dragon I am, whose second nature it is to share...I am going to teach you how to figure this relationship out. If I learn that either of you has done the other in, and caused pain to those I care about, I'll be the one to eviscerate the survivor and light his entrails on fire. Got it?"

"How dare you speak down to me like that! I saved yer asses when you came over here with yer tails tucked, hiding from Crimson!" Kieran yelled, spit flying.

"And we've more than paid you for that service! Thank you for reminding me I'm only a tool for you. It wasn't out of friendship that you've helped us, and we've helped you, huh? You saw the profit of having two dragons do your bidding, eh?" The dragon squatted in front of Kieran and the two stared long and hard at one another.

"Devon? He's my friend. And Gareth? He loves my dragon-mate, and she loves him. Derek? Yeah, I trust him like I would my own. And they would be completely heartbroken if either of you died at the other's hands and teeth - or if Helena finally ends up at her last straw one day and gives up. So, for them and for her, I do this. I dare speak to you like this - so ...you ...will ...listen."

"He will not listen to you any more than he listens to any others. Kieran does what he likes. If he loved Helena half as much as he keeps saying he does, he wouldn't shame her by being so damned obvious with his prowling." Argoth glared at Kieran, "Don't you realize you're only making yourself look bad and hurting Helena in the process?"

"That's because he doesn't understand love. He's never felt love as you have, Argoth. That's the Goddess' fault, not his, not Helena's, and not yours."

Kieran raised a shaggy brow. But he said nothing. The dragon went on.

"You're doing all of this for spite, but it's not helping. You knew she had a mate and took the chance. Kieran, you lost. Accept it. Stop trying to be petty. Someday, you'll know what it is to feel love so strongly that you can't stop yourself from doing anything you can to get back to the one you love. And you'll know it's true when they return love to you in the same way. This is not that time, Kieran. This is a time you will have to survive through - until love finds you. So, listen. And if you follow my advice, the rest of this situation should follow through properly."

Senias stood up and looked between the two of them. "Will you listen to me?" Senias asked. He waited as the Alpha glared at Argoth and then scowled at him. No one moved. No one said anything. And then...

"Go ahead," Kieran whispered.

"Helena and Argoth have a haven that is away from all others so that their time spent together is a secret. You need to have the same. You need to find a secret place for your time together with other women, and you should trust those women not to say anything about their time with you. Make sure they are trustworthy. I can give you some names and places for such things. You need to have a release? - this is how you do it. Do not get another lycan caught up, but then, you know better than that. You're going to be discreet. And when you come back together, no questions and no questioning yourselves. You're all making the best of an awkward situation that none of you can get out of for now. Simple. And if you find love, Kieran, remember that you still have a mate, and you are bound to her until you both can still be true to your packs and family. You're both in the same boat."

Kieran huffed, but he listened. Senias turned to the other man.

"What are you doing for your mate, Argoth? Leia knows about all of this? How are you working with that?" Senias asked.

"I've never lied to her. When she met me, she knew my heart was Helena's. I am discreet, out of respect for my mate as well. She's been a friend and confidante. Leia won't look at others, though I've told her if she is just as discreet and treated well, I won't deny her. She won't leave, though I've offered to set her up with her Pack and remain her mate in name. She won't take our pups from me, which I am grateful for. Other than that, she doesn't push or demand anything."

"You have a shared family, whether you like it or not. This happens a lot with dragons, but we don't have to keep things quiet. You need to accept it." So, like Kieran, Argoth had sought someone to share life with and raise children with. The only difference was that he had given his mate a choice. Senias looked at Kieran. "It's been years. Accept it. Treat her with respect for what she has done for everyone. Go to the ones I point you toward and be discreet. Stop getting angry with them for something they can't help. One day, you'll understand it. And when you do, you're going to look back on this and how you've acted these past few years and you'll be ashamed. Do better. Make up for it. Don't make me come back here and kick your ass." Senias brushed himself off. "I'll leave my journal on your bed. The information you need will be there."

"That it?" Kieran asked.

"That's it." Senias took a step back and watched the two pathetic looking lycan do their best not to speak to one another or look at one another. The dragon rolled his eyes. "I'm going back inside to enjoy my drunken stupor."

"Alpha!" The yell had them all pausing. The voice was especially problematic for Kieran. The big Alpha stepped forward to face the elder blacksmith.

"Noran, why've ya come so far from yer village? I thought you weren't interested in the ceremonial mating celebration. What's happening?"

Everyone took notice of Helena trailing the older lycan.

"Have ya not noticed your mate's maid is gone all these days?" Noran asked, a whine leaving his chest.

"To be honest, I figured my mate had sent her packing like she does with any she assumes I've had relations with. I have a very jealous woman..."

"Had nothin' ta do with yer cock, Alpha!" the male spat at Kieran with contempt in his eyes. "My daughter, the one you tug along? She's been gone all the week! I thought she'd stayed over ta help with the celebration, but I found this at the forest's edge." Noran showed Kieran the lovely wolf pendant he had carved for his lover.

"She wouldn't have parted with such a prize willingly." Senias pointed out. "Did you end things with her or...?"

"I ended things with her." Helena made her way to them all. "I only came because I'm worried about Tasha and about our pups. I let Tasha go when she had the nerve to wear that to work. That was a week ago. I've not seen her since she left that morning before I came to you to braid your beads."

"You sure you didn't take the challenge?" It wasn't unheard of for another lycan to challenge those who had a mate bond when they thought they had a chance. Had Helena finally reached her limit and sent someone to the fields?

"There was no challenge to be had. I sent her home, and she left, still wearing that. If she had challenged me, you'd have all known." Helena's pleading eyes took in those of her mate. "If not me..."

"Elves," Kieran growled as his fingers and thumb moved over the wooden pendant.

CHAPTER TWENTY-ONE

A CALL TO ARMS

SENIAS CAME OUT OF the cabin shaking his head.

"They made it here. I smell both Devon and his mate and the fresh scents of the paints we placed upon them," Kieran acknowledged.

"They moved nothing inside. They didn't make it far. And if those that took them were smart, they could've easily crossed through the forest where the hunt was happening." Senias pointed out.

"Half the damn young-uns of the pack trampled over their tracks for the night's hunt. Damn... what if the elves are out there with those pups? Not all of 'em have been well-trained." Kieran was rumbling his anger as he moved from the cabin to backtrack the direction Devon and Eva should have come. "If they were here, I don't smell a trail leading them off. Did they use magic?"

"We don't know that it's elves, yet. We don't even know if Tasha got taken by elves. What if she was just angry and ripped the thing off?" Senias pointed out.

"She wouldn't have."

Senias turned to look at Helena, who had come here with them. He was at a loss for what he should say or do right then. Had he been wrong? The elves had been leaving. The way they had destroyed Pack Rourke spoke of retribution...and that was usually the last strike in any war that the dragon had witnessed or fought. It made no sense for the elves to attack again.

"Tasha cares about Kieran. For her, it's more than just sex and she wanted to be part of his life for a long time. The carving says my mate gives a shit about her, too."

"Helena..." Kieran began, but Helena held up her hand to force him to stop. This woman, the Alpha of their pack, was very much that. She was a true queen of her people, despite her relationship pitfalls. She commanded respect, even from her mate, despite their circumstances.

"As I was saying, she wouldn't have thrown it away so easily. She either did it to get his attention or someone took it off." Helena let it sink in when she heard someone coming through the woods.

Kieran and Senias stepped in front of her, just in case. Instead of an enemy, Argoth and Derek came bursting through from the upper hill and slid down to where the others were. They shifted to their human forms, and their expressions set the mood.

"I tracked Gareth. There were footprints surrounding where he had skidded and moved and tried to evade people in his wolf form. Inea was there, but she was with the shaman. She wasn't responding. Had some sort of blue foam coming from her mouth."

"No... dragon's bane..." Senias didn't wait. He created a small portal the size of a doorway. "Let's go." Argoth looked at Kieran.

"What do we do?" His bright blue eyes shimmered with pent-up frustration. His son's expression matched.

"We collect our troops, collect our dragons, and we go after the bastards. We already know where their camps are supposed ta be. I'm tired of this, give and take! They've taken enough!" Kieran roared as he turned to shift and run through the portal. Derek was right behind him.

Argoth paused, and he looked to Helena. His eyes searched hers. "I'll bring them back. I brought Devon back to you and now I'll bring both our pups back."

"See that they are all alive and well when you bring them back to me. I want all of my pups back, Argoth." Helena was shaking. "Watch him. Don't let him get them killed for some stupid vengeance." He went through the portal and Helena was the last to step through before the dragon.

"SHE CONFIRMED IT WAS elves," Senias said as he came out of the large, rounded structure. "They wanted Gareth, not her."

"Is she coming?" Kieran asked and then found himself with a furious Senias grabbing him by the beard to tug his face down. He growled but didn't react more than that.

"She got hit with dragon's bane. When it's mixed correctly, it forces a dragon into a painful reaction. Your shaman is about to have her taken out of the tent so she can shift into her dragon form because she can barely hold her human one. She can't think straight, Kieran. No..." He shoved the big Alpha backward. "She won't be going."

"Why're you pissed off at me? The elves are the ones that did it. And now they have my pups. Put yer anger and rage on them, Scales." Kieran spat. "After all, you said we didn't need ta worry about the elves no more."

Senias took off running away from them and then jumped into the air, a flash of light telling them all that he was shifting. The creature he became was nearly half the size of one of the castle towers. The dark dragon nearly disappeared into the night. All three lycan looked at one another, then silently ran in the same direction, shifting as they did. Their pack guards then followed suit. The howl that Kieran put into the air once he reached the gates would put everyone on alert and have the others calling everyone in from the hunt. More and more capable lycan joined their Alpha in a new hunt.

Helena watched as they all left. The Lady Alpha had already handled her duties. Kieran had been quick with calling in the younger lycan from the hunt. She made sure the palace was prepared for any injuries incoming. She had the kitchen make more good food. Now, she made her way behind their shaman to watch as they carried Inea to the river. She stood back when the beautiful blonde sorceress shifted in a flash of light to an equally beautiful dragon. Her scales were pale with subtle greens and blues. The Lady Alpha had never really seen the dragons so close. Her eyes moved over the scaled being, her steady breathing seen at her sides, the wings pressed close to her back. Helena reached her hand out, wanting to feel the ...skin?

"I'd not do that without permission, Alpha. She is very defensive right now." The voice came from the shaman, Chaunice, who had served this pack right after she had become a member. She smiled and Helena realized she at least understood her curiosity.

"I wanted to ask her if she could feel my pup. He was quite attached to her, and I hoped that maybe if there was any way Inea could feel him, and let me know anything..."

"The dragon told us she couldn't focus. She couldn't find Gareth. The spellwork and the poison they used on her, it was well-researched and though it did less than intended, it did enough." Chaunice moved forward and, using a large spoon, she scooped the mixture she had with her into a wooden bowl, into the nostril of the dragon.

"Less than intended? Looks like it did enough." Helena grimaced and shivered as she watched what the shaman did. The dragon coughed and swallowed and then stilled to continue to sleep. Inea's claws dug into the earth where she was, and her closest eye barely flinched.

"The concoction that they poisoned her with? It killed her. We brought her back with the other dragon's help."

"Chaunice! The boy is awake!" The apprentice yelled from the tent, where both shamans treated the wounded. Helena went running into the tent with Chaunice. She wasn't a shaman, but she was a mother and had been a friend to Rory's parents. His survival was a miracle of the Goddess.

Inside, the boy, who was but an adolescent, was being held by one apprentice while Chaunice began talking to him softly in the old lycan. The growls and rumbles from all of his caregivers were helping to calm his nerves. Helena came close and when he turned to see her, she wiped a tear from his face.

"I'm so sorry, Rory. We didn't know your pack was in danger. We thought the elves had moved on. I...we can never make up for that. But you will always have a place with Pack Weylyn. We will take care of you and make sure you have a mentor and—"

"No elves..." the boy whispered, his voice hoarse.

"No, there are no elves here. We wouldn't—"

"No. I...didn't see elves. Not that night. The guard... they hid me, ma'am. When I came out, they were all gone," He started crying. "Then the elves came. So, I hid again. Like a coward. But the door jammed."

Helena's gaze matched the expression of others in the room. "Not elves? Rory...who killed your mama and papa?" She put a hand on his cheek. "This is very important. If you can tell me, you may save my own pups."

"Lycan. They...they were another pack. Ma and Pa were hosting for 'em. But I don't remember who. I just wanted ta go play with my friends. Are...are my friends dead, too?"

"I hope not. We're still searching for all of them. Rory, you are not a coward. You did everything you could. If you had come out, you'd be dead, too. And the Goddess has plans for you. Thank you for telling us." Helena leaned over and kissed his forehead before nodding to the shaman. She backed away, shock over her face.

The Lady Alpha turned and began running for the dragoness. Taking a chance, she moved her fingers over the scales of the dragon's lower face and then moved her hands up to get to Inea's eye. There was skin here, skin that could feel things better than in other areas. Her hands moved over that warm skin, and she spoke calmly.

"If you love him, reach out to him."

~ That's not how it works. ~

Helena gasped and jumped back, holding her head as she felt the voice move through her mind. She'd experienced this with Senias, but Inea caught her off-guard. She stumbled and fell to the ground as the dragoness raised her head to look down at the woman.

~ I can reach out. I can coax him to come awake, for he's not conscious. But I cannot pinpoint exactly where he is unless he can truly concentrate and so can I. My mind is having trouble focusing. I'm not sure where I might cast a portal to, even if I could. ~

"Okay, okay, just... stop talking to me... let me catch up." She rested on her hands back on the ground behind her where she sat.

"Devon must get that from you," Inea whispered. She had shifted and was now crouched in front of Helena. "Sorry. I'm yet weak. Tell me. Tell me what has happened."

"They left to find Eva and our boys, and I don't know where they are. I cannot just stand by and do nothing. Especially not now. It wasn't the elves, Inea. The pup you all rescued? He said it wasn't elves. It was lycan. They're going after the wrong enemy. I think...I think someone betrayed us all."

Inea's mouth was agape. Licking her lips, she sat on her hip and took some breaths. "I...I need you to keep me going. There might be a way to make my connection stronger. We'll need a shallow platter, round is best, water, a candle, and your blood."

"You're still weak. Can you mindspeak to your mate? Let them know?" Helena asked.

"It's one or the other." The two women held gazes for only two seconds. No words were necessary.

CHAPTER TWENTY-TWO

ON THE RUN

IT TOOK KIERAN, ARGOTH, and Derek quite a while, moving outward from the cabin to find the trail. And when that happened, Senias, who felt rather useless at the moment, took his human position on Kieran's lupine back. Holding on to the neck and keeping himself in place with his legs as the enormous wolf barreled through the forest to the north of the main packlands. The canopy was too dense and the underbrush too tangled for his dragon form.

~ If we don't catch up in time... ~ Kieran thought as he came to a halt.

"We will find them! Stop thinking we won't!" Senias snapped. He couldn't help it. He and Devon had just become good friends after all these years of being around one another, and he didn't want to lose that. And Gareth...if Gareth went off on anyone, would they kill him? Sen shook his head.

Derek shifted. "You can't guarantee that." He could hear several of the other lycan halt behind them, but they hadn't shifted yet.

"They'll be fine." Argoth had shifted forms to talk to his son while the two a short distance ahead of them snapped at each other. "Gareth's a brawler like you. I mean, look how often he gets out of tight spots with you. Of course, there's Devon and we both know he'll be tryin' to get his new mate free before anything else. He's a force to be reckoned with when he gets started." Argoth wasn't sure if he was trying to convince Derek that his friends were okay or if he was trying to convince himself.

Senias concentrated on Devon. He wasn't sure if he'd be able to feel his friend or not. He had before. But they had always been in close enough proximity. The dragon realized Devon was unconscious, dead, or not near. He didn't like any of those scenarios. When Kieran continued to the top of a gully, Senias went with him. They could both hear the movement of their feet on a trail.

"I don't feel them," Senias looked at the marching elves below. It surprised him that the elves had not heard them. The draconic man turned to the Alpha. ~ Don't... ~

Kieran leapt from the side of the gully, right into the middle of the Elven contingent, making their way up to the last pass before heading into their own lands. He was howling and growling and began slashing, going into his hybrid form to be more efficient. Senias slid down the side of the gully and went into the battle along with the other guards that were following them.

"Fuck!" Senias came off the enraged lycan and rolled away, facing not one, but two armed Elven guards. He couldn't shift yet, but he could defend himself well enough. Grabbing the halberd that was headed his way, he then let go with his stronger arm to grab the incoming dagger. He jerked the halberd and kicked the incomer in the groin, taking his dagger as well.

Looking down at the mess of fighting bodies, Argoth shook his head and stepped back to devise a plan.

"Shift! Take 'em out!" Kieran roared behind Senias.

"It's too tight! And I don't have claws like you, dumbass!" Senias grabbed the halberd and started using it to beneficial effect at least! He looked over his shoulder to see if Argoth and Derek were around.

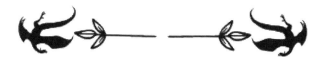

MEANWHILE, WITH DEREK BY his side, Argoth ran along the top of the gully. He looked over at his eldest before shifting to his human form. "We'll work our way down the side and see if we can't find any trace of Devon, Eva, or Gareth. Stay close to me and use yer wolf. It'll catch their scents better. Howl if ya find anything. But don't get away from me pup, I don't need to explain that to yer mama."

"Don't worry about me. I've always had the Goddess' luck on my side." With that, Derek shifted back into his wolf form and did as his father asked.

Going into hybrid form, Argoth led Derek down the side of the gully and started his attack from the back of the elves. It was an unexpected attack. Every elf he fought; the experienced warrior drew in a lung full of their scent to see if he could catch a hint of their friends.

When he finally fought his way to Senias and Kieran, it was to call out, "Not... here!" His muzzle snarled as he slashed and knocked the next few elves back away from the dragon to give him more room to work. "Need some alive to talk." He spoke to the dragon more than to Kieran because, of the two, the dragon seemed more reasonable.

"Make them understand that!" Senias yelled as he continued to defend himself as best he could. He wound up behind Argoth instead of Kieran because the big Alpha was getting surrounded.

"I smell the herbs from the ceremony! The trail leads into the forest across the road!" Derek said as he shifted and grabbed an incoming sword blade between his hands and then made a move to disarm the elf who had tried to cut him.

Argoth knew that this wasn't right. Something about this entire situation seemed off. That the elves were more intent on Kieran than any of them didn't elude him, either. However, Derek's words were like an affirmation of the previous idea. Were the pups there? He was about to find out.

"Cover us!" Kieran ordered.

"What?!" Senias watched Argoth leave, then Kieran heaved a bunch of the elves from him and took off to follow. "Cover us...right..." Senias was fed up. He had already had too many close calls. So, he made his way to the middle of the road, where he had the maximum space for his huge dragon form. And he shifted.

His dark-scaled bulk slammed several elves to the ground. His ass and tail threw others further away by their sudden appearance.

"Well, that'll definitely cover 'em!" Derek yelled. Both he and the dragon continued battling, trying to keep most of the elves busy.

THERE WERE SEVERAL HORSES out there tied to trees and a small tent. The scent of the celebration spices that would have been on Devon and Eva's bodies emanated from that area. As Argoth made his way closer, a net enfolded him and tugged him up off the ground.

He let out a yelp of surprise before struggling to sit up better. Argoth had been in hybrid form when the net hit him and took him up to hang between several trees. He couldn't get free enough to see where Kieran was or where the elves were!

"Kieran! It's a trap! It's a trap!" Argoth yelled. "I see clothes from the celebration! That was the lure!"

"Means they know where my pups are!" Kieran growled as he considered helping Argoth down. He immediately began looking for others. An arrow hit his upper flank, and, with a sharp whine, he ran to the other side of the wagon to take cover.

"You wanted this fight so bad that you slaughtered my people to get it, cur! Come out and face your punishment!" A tall, well-made elf came walking out from the tree line on the opposite side of the clearing. The horses neighed and popped hooves on the ground nervously as they tried to get free of the tense situation.

Twisting around as best he could, Argoth looked towards where the elves were as he called out, "Slaughtered, yer people? Ya took ours first before we ever got here!" He tried to cut through the netting with an extended claw.

Argoth got an arrow into his palm for his trouble. The sound he made covered Kieran's snapping of the arrow in his own shoulder. The big Alpha bit back a pained grunt and, shifting, he moved into the woods to take out any that were around. Argoth was a talker, so he let the man do what he did best.

"We owe you! We were trying to leave; even cleaned up your dead! Kept them from becoming poison until you could send them to your fields! And what do we get in return? You kill us like it's a sport! Well, I'll take your children for my children!" The largest elf was moving constantly, trying to find Kieran. He moved to the wagon where the lycan had been hiding. He kicked the leavings of the arrow and watched for signs from the thick forest.

"Yer children..." Argoth had to snap the arrow. He growled and snarled as he yanked the rest free and dropped it to the ground. It took him only a moment to put it all together while his hand healed.

"You'll never find them! My ethics may keep me from killing them as you've killed mine, but you will never have them again!" He knocked another arrow and was drawing the string back. He turned to let the arrow fly as Kieran leapt into the air to take him down.

Argoth watched Kieran take the elf down and let his breath out, "Don't! Don't..." The cries and the sounds of breaking bones told him he was too late.

Kieran came up, blood all over him. He growled, the hybrid form of the wolf a sight of horror. He had the elf's arrow in his right chest, the shaft of another in his shoulder, and a dagger in his upper back. The Alpha reached back and ripped out with a harsh grunt.

Argoth stared at Kieran in stunned silence. When he finally found his tongue, he asked what was foremost on his mind. "Tell me ya didn't do that? That he was talking about some other Pack?" Argoth was fighting the netting again.

"What? They fuckin took out Pack Rourke and you think I wouldn't take out a camp of the pointy-eared fuckers when I had the chance?" The Alpha got the rest of the wood out of him and used the dagger to cut the rigging. Argoth dropped like a load of rocks. But the scout wasn't free yet.

"They... I didn't know we were taking out the entire damned bunch for the actions of some!" Argoth snarled once he regained his breath and started trying to get free of the netting now that he was on the ground.

"It was practical. They were still deep enough in the packlands ta be a danger. And if you don't think they're a danger, did ya forget why we're out here? They took our pups!" Kieran growled.

"Ya don't..." Argoth paused in what he was saying as he realized what Kieran had said. "Our...?" The old scout's eyes grew large and his struggle more desperate. "Kieran—" This entire moment had just taken a dangerous turn, and he knew it.

"I'm no idiot. You think I don't know good timing when I see it? Or incongruent timing? When a child comes too early? Has the wrong look?" Kieran watched Argoth struggle to get himself free. His amber eyes shimmered, and he lingered around the other lycan without helping. His snout snarled as he considered the situation. "And speaking of good timing..."

CHAPTER TWENTY-THREE

THE RESCUE

THE WORLD HAD SPUN. Eva wasn't used to shifting. That had thrown her. The rest? Even worse. She felt something in the pit of her stomach. Slowly, her eyes opened. She was in a cage. The dreaded cage that they all tried their best to avoid. At least the hay was fresh. Though, it was not comfortable considering the barely-there clothing she had on. She looked down at her bare legs and the smeared paint.

"Devon?" Eva got up to her knees quickly, scanning the encampment. They were in a thick portion of the forest, two boulders cut them off from one side. She could see the other cages. Each one was big as a wagon. Actually...they were wagons. She could hear horses nearby.

Devon was in one of the larger wagons and though the shackles he wore prevented him from shifting, they didn't prevent him from assuring his mate that he was fine. He rumbled for her as he moved to test the gate on the cage again. "I hoped I'd been wrong the first few times I tried. I got a headache. Can't hardly think. Otherwise, I think I'll make it." His gaze looked towards her cage. "These gates ain't opening, so I'm guessing' they're made for our kind."

There were other wagons with cages on the back of them. Not just their own. This was what a slaving caravan looked like. The cages weren't always necessary, but Eva had known they were for a purpose. She'd never seen this many in Madron Regis' old caravan, though.

"No. They're magically locked. Only Regis has the keys." At least, that was how it had always been before. Eva wasn't sure now. Her eyes scanned the area further out behind them. There were guards. They seemed on edge.

~ GARETH? ~ INEA'S voice came to Gar's head faintly, but he could tell it wasn't a dream.

Unlike his older brother, Gareth was slower to come around and when he did, it was to Inea's voice in the fuzz of his head. ~ Mmm-hmm? ~ He felt like he was waking from one hell of a night of drinking moonwyne. Something told him that wasn't the case.

~ I need you to focus on me. I'm going to use our connection to come to you. What will we be facing? We need to know what's happening. Quickly. This is...this is taxing. ~

It was what Eva said next that had Gareth reacting quicker. As he shook his head to clear it and was up and, on his feet, he heard her speaking.

"I know this place. They're taking us to the Underground Portal. There's no telling where we'll end up if we don't get out of here." Eva was looking around frantically, trying to figure out a plan. "Have anything? Can you get out, Gar?"

Rubbing a hand over his face, Gareth focused his blue eyes on the surroundings outside his cage and saw Eva looking his way. He held a finger to his lips and rubbed his temple to let her know he was talking with Inea. ~ We're in a slaver's caravan, magic sealed cages and there are several of 'em. Not sure how many guards are with it. The scent is familiar. Can't place it yet though. My head's still foggy. ~ Gareth had to stop the connection when the world started spinning. He knew Inea would wait for more from him.

As the light of day was going down, the tents were being set up.

"Gar?" Eva held the bars as she looked over at the cage he was in.

"Hey! Hush up there! We'll put up the covers over your pens if ya keep it up!" The guard banged on Eva's cage with the club he carried. She jumped back away from the cage door, growling in response.

Devon's hands gripped his own bars as his golden gaze narrowed on the slaver that was threatening his mate. He growled in a way that promised the guard there'd be nothing to stop Devon from ripping him to pieces if he got free.

There was a different rumble from Gareth as he let Eva know he was okay. Whatever they had hit him with just packed a hell of a punch.

~ I know it hurts. But focus on me as well as the place you think I should make the portal near you. Please, Gareth...help me help you... ~

Turning to look out the bars on the back side of the wagon he was in, he felt the guard walk over his way and so he loosened the front flap of his pants and reached in to grab his cock. "Gotta pee. Yer not into that sorta shit, are ya?" He shrugged his shoulders as he turned back towards the back bars to relieve himself. "I mean, if ya are, then watch all ya like."

"Filth." The guard turned away and walked back toward where another caged wagon was sitting to check on the occupant.

Gar chuckled, then let Inea see the stretch of forest not far from his wagon's backside. ~ Tree line out of sight, so far, I see eight, but there's probably twice that if this is the slavers I know. It also means there's a group of ten, a good stretch ahead of the caravan, and a group of ten a good stretch behind it to prevent raiders from takin' the camp. ~

~ We're on the way. ~ Inea's voice became a whisper in his mind.

Gareth became nauseated and as he tucked himself away, his eyes squeezed shut for a moment. The connection ebbed away. Apparently, they'd know about his connection to a dragon because he could not keep the mental chat going for too long. If Inea was still out there...what had happened?

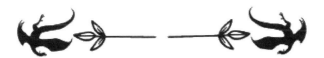

THE CAVERN WAS LIT up with several wall torches. The two women were on the large golden floor to one side of that cavern. Inea was on her knees in the liquid metal, while Helena stood in front of her. There were candles lit in a circle around them and Inea sat with her head bowed and eyes closed. Suddenly, the dragoness gasped.

Inea looked at Helena and nodded. She held her hand out to the lycan woman. The golden floor she had been drawing energy from was in her mate's lair. Inea's smile was a sample of hope.

"He showed me. The spell worked. The aurumn floor worked. I have the energy now. But I will not have this to use for coming back. Are you ready?" Inea let Helena help her up from her knees.

"Yes, let's go get my pups, Lady Inea." Helena was eager to have her sons and Eva back where they belonged. If the servant was there, well, Helena would let her come back with them too.

Inea held out her hand and focused. Magical energy rose from the floor they were standing on to surround the blonde woman's body and then pushed outward from her palm to create a portal. In the swirling blue mist within a door-sized space before them, they could see forest trails in the new morning's light. It was on the other side of the doorway. "Go. Quietly."

"I will never get accustomed to such things," Helena whispered as she went through first. She took her hybrid form and crouched to wait for Inea to join her. Her dark red and gold fur made it easy to blend into the foliage. They remained where they were until they caught sight of the first guard making his rounds.

The guard slammed his club into the last wagon cage and the growl that came back at him had the man laughing. "You get to sleep when we tell you to sleep, bitch. You're making my life shit, so you don't get to rest." He turned around to come face to face with Helena.

In her hybrid form, Helena was a few inches taller than he was and she quickly had him in her grasp and pinned, so that he couldn't call out for help.

As soon as she shoved the guard into the cage, an arm came around his neck from that cage. The prisoner lifted him up from the ground.

"Where's the key?" Helena snarled as her eyes lit up. She was searching the male's pockets looking for the tiny piece of metal.

"Alpha? Around his wrist." Tasha waited until the lady had the keys and she snapped the guard's neck. She let the dead guard go from her grasp. She was shocked to see Helena away from the palace.

Reverting to her human form, Helena brushed her hair back and looked at the maid within the cage. "Don't look so surprised. My pups are in danger, and I won't lose any more to the fields." She retrieved the key and moved to unlock the cage. Turning towards the dragoness, she tossed the key over so Inea could free Gareth. Then they'd see Devon and Eva freed as well.

"I wasn't sure you'd know. The ones that grabbed me...I couldn't tell who they were. I...I've seen elves and slavers and I hate ta say it, but...I think they were lycan."

"Lycan? I only saw the slaver and his people. He owed Kieran for having his caravan raided after he had purchased me," Eva explained.

Helena rumbled to get the woman to continue as she looked Devon over while Inea saw to free Gareth and looked him over.

"Yes, ma'am. I overheard them talking. The slaver's mad. Said he blamed Pack Weylyn. And the elves? Well, a bunch of 'em that were retreating? Our pack killed them. Or some pack killed them. But they blamed Weylyn. And the lycan? I don't know, other than they said something about there being secrets and dishonor all over the pack because of the Alphas. I..." Tasha's eyes hit the ground. "So sorry for my part, ma'am," she looked up at Helena sheepishly. "But I don't know why it would make a person want ta hurt ya so bad as ta take yer pups. You lead proper. That's all that should matter."

Devon's brow drew down and as his mother checked him out, he put to memory what Tasha was telling them because it needed to be investigated once they were all home.

Once Gareth could get out of his cage, Inea held him in her arms and looked him over. "Are you okay? You just...you were down and then you were gone."

"I'm alright, just knocked me out and stunned me so my head was a mess, but it's better now." Gareth looked the dragoness over in return, "I'm more worried about you. Are ya alright? I tried to reach ya when they hit us, but I couldn't get to ya. It was bad. What happened?" His hand rested on Inea's cheek as he nuzzled her and breathed her scent in just to make certain that she truly was alright.

"I'm better. They hit me with dragons' bane. But Derek and Argoth found me quick enough. Your mother helped me get to the aurumn and helped me find you. I'm healing." Inea put her hand on his cheek and looked into his beautiful eyes.

The blue of his eyes lit up as he looked at all the other cages. "We need to get everyone free and get 'em outta here."

"Collum? Ya gonna get some grub?!" Madron Regis yelled from the side of the tented area. "Yer not taking a leak are you, some guard you are." He chuckled, the sound telling the escapees that he was moving toward them.

At the sound of Madron Regis' voice, Eva turned and growled, shifting partially into a defensive stance. Tasha did the same but took a defensive stance in front of her Alpha.

Moving into the shadows, Devon went into his hybrid form and waited for the slaver to move past him toward his mother, mate, brother, and friend.

"Oh, was that his name? Sorry, but he won't need to partake in any further meals." Helena stood with the two females before her and looked right at the slaver.

"Who the fuck are you?" Regis pulled his switchblade and readied himself.

"Don't know who I am? You should. You took my pups, hurt our friend, and thought you'd get away with it. Never underestimate a mother or what she'll do for her young. I promise you'll never make that mistake again." The sweet-natured female gave the disgusting man a vicious smile as her eldest moved to tower over him from behind.

CHAPTER TWENTY-FOUR

TEMPTATIONS

KIERAN CIRCLED THE DOWNED lycan even after the elves that had netted Argoth were called away. He growled as Argoth struggled, the hackles on his neck rising. It'd be so simple. His rival would be gone, he could blame the elves, and they might even consider him the hero for trying his best. No one would know. And he got the feeling, as Argoth shifted in front of him, still struggling, that the other wolf understood his own predicament.

The hair down his spine stood on end as Argoth watched Kieran circle him. Shifting to his human form again, he tried to pull at the netting while also waiting for that death blow to come from the Alpha male. They both knew it was what Kieran wanted to do. Argoth had the one thing that Kieran wanted the most in this world. He had Helena's heart and her love.

It was never that easy, was it? Kieran would never let someone confuse him with a truly honorable sort. But he knew he could never live with himself if he did this. As easy as it might make his life? As easy as it would be to handle this once and for all, the big Alpha couldn't end his rival's life.

Shifting back to his hybrid form, he went to Argoth and began cutting the straps from the sides so the other man could get out.

Once he could get free of the net, Argoth stumbled back in absolute shock. "Thank you, I…"

"Not doing it for you. Don't flatter yerself." Kieran helped the man up and then turned to the sounds of new howls outside of the thick forest. He recognized them! "Devon!"

"Gareth! Helena…" Argoth's heart leaped every bit as far as Kieran's did. The two shared a momentary glance at one another before heading back to the fight.

Devon was in hybrid form, and he was keeping the elves back from his mate, brother, and mother while the dragons worked at the stragglers. But his mother was having none of it as she lunged at the next male that dared try to harm one of her pups! Helena gave as good as she got.

The gray and white wolf was on the chest of one slaver as she took him down to the ground and buried her teeth in his throat. He gurgled as he thrashed to get free.

As Kieran and Argoth came to the outer border of the clearing that their dragon friend had expanded with his bulk, they could see Devon, Gareth, Helena, Tasha, and Eva all in their wolf and hybrid forms jumping into the battle.

Argoth ran in, not caring about any repercussions he may face from the Alpha as he jumped in to help.

When Helena caught sight of Kieran, she shifted forms and rushed right at him, only to feel Devon's arm grab her and tug her back. Her son was in his hybrid form and was much stronger. The look she gave Kieran told her mate that she knew exactly why this had happened and that once again he was at fault for the near loss of her pups!

"What the .... Helena?!" Kieran felt lost as his mate nearly attacked him.

"Mama, stay close to Eva. I don't want ya hurt. We'll handle that later!" Devon rumbled gently to her as her glare turned back on him, but it quickly softened as she nodded in agreement to ease him enough to let her go.

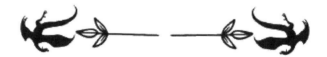

"HALT!" INEA, WHO WAS also in her dragon form, used the only word she could create with her mouth that might get them to stop fighting. She wasn't sure how to make it stop without either group giving in. There were more elves than lycan, but the lycan with the dragons were formidable fighters. And Senias was in full battle mode. ~ Stop fighting them! The elves didn't kill Pack Rourke! We were right! They were on their way out! Let them leave! ~

~ They were part of this. They took Devon and Eva! ~ Senias roared and sent another gout of fiery breath toward more of the elves that had gathered to the side and struck him with arrows.

~ Devon and Eva are safe! So is Gar! ~ Inea tried to push Senias physically to get him to stop. His mind was such a fog that it frightened her, a fear Gareth could also feel.

Taking her human form, Helena gave her own howl since her mate would not be calling a halt to this nonsense. The howl she gave was just as commanding as Kieran could be. She pushed past Devon's enormous form to snarl at the next group of elves that came their way! "I said enough! No more of this!" To make her point, the female Alpha that never acted as anything, but the Lady of the Pack grabbed the front of the shirt of the next elf and simply shoved him back into the group of others. "The next lycan that draws blood, I swear, will answer to me! Now I said stop!"

"What are ya doin'? We've almost got them done! They're not innocent in this!" Kieran yelled at his mate with a loud gnashing of his teeth and a growl in his chest.

"And neither are you!" Helena snapped right back at him. ~Senias! Stop this! Please, it isn't their fault! ~ She tried reaching out to the dragon even as the elves fell back. One of their own gave them the command to stand down.

Instead of looking at Kieran to help with the dragon, Helena turned to her son. "Devon, reach out to him and get him to stop. What they did was wrong, but it was in response to what your own father did. Please try to call him off."

"It's not his dragon!" Kieran was breathing hard and turned to push the halt with his mind as well. But then he staggered back as the big black and maroon dragon roared and, in a fit of rage, turned to face the big Alpha.

Helena watched in horror as what Senias had warned them of unfolded before her eyes. The dragon was down on his haunches, his forward feet moving toward Kieran. The gigantic creature was stalking the Alpha.

"Everybody get back!" Kieran took a step away from his family and his people. The dragon's eyes darted to the side, but then the Alpha howled and made a barking and growling sound. It was old lycan, a jeer to get the dragon's attention on him. And it worked. The dragon's frills shivered, and he growled. His head moved toward Kieran and the lycan had to maneuver quickly to be missed by those dagger-sized teeth and the liquid flame that still dripped from its mouth.

Inea moved her wings out to protect anyone who took shelter beneath them. Both lycan and elves were taking cover together at this point.

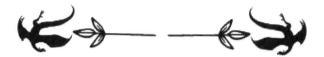

"Devon... your father is wrong. Senias isn't anyone's dragon. He's your friend, remember? He's the pack's defender... but he's your friend. Try to stop this." Eva squeezed her mate's hand. "Remember! You make his darkness into light!"

Devon stared into Eva's eyes for what felt like a week but was only a few moments. Then, with a quick nod, he turned from her to get closer to the dark-colored dragon.

~ Senias, we need to get out of here and ya need to stop! We are okay now and if ya keep up, our own Pack will get caught in the flames. ~ Devon urged his friend without commanding or demanding it from him. Sen didn't belong to him like a pet. They were friends, and he respected Senias for all the help he had been. Devon wasn't sure what his mother meant, but he was certain that if they could get things settled, he'd find out soon enough.

The dragon growled, his head moving quickly to the side. His blue-green eyes shimmered, and he roared at where everyone was standing. Kieran made a move, grabbing the dragon by his left frill and nostril. Senias moved his head up and then slung the Alpha into the ground with a burst of flame before placing a full-sized claw over the man, pinning him.

~ "Sen, don't! For me please!" ~ Devon broke away from the others to move closer to show his friend that he didn't fear him. He calmed himself while getting to the dragon's enormous head and snout. He was getting closer to where his father was being pinned. Lifting one of his own hands out, he didn't grab the dragon as Kieran had. Instead, he placed his palm against the hard snout and closed his eyes, putting his complete trust in his friend. ~ "It's okay, we're all safe and we're gonna go home. I need ya to calm down, my friend, can ya do that for me?" ~ He rumbled softly while keeping his hand on Sen's snout. It wasn't about command and obedience; it was about faith and trust. He wanted Sen to understand that he had that.

~ Devon... ~ Senias raised his clawed hand from Kieran's chest and took a step back. The big Alpha took a deep breath and started to cough. His right arm was hanging limp and the dragon's breath had burned a good portion of his body. But he was alive.

~ "Yeah Sen, it's me." ~ Devon pulled his friend's attention away from his father and onto himself while others rushed in to help Kieran.

~ You're alive. Your mate? Gar? The elves...did not harm you? ~ Senias purred and the sound of hissing deep in his throat and chest told Devon that the dragon's flames were being extinguished. Smoke blew from his nostrils and then the air cleared before the gigantic creature took a clear breath.

Slowly, Devon shook his head as he kept his hand on the skin just between the dragon's snout and eyes. He wanted Sen to focus on him. ~ "We're alright, they just knocked us out." ~

"I believe..." Eva walked up behind Devon and placed a hand on her mate's shoulder while she looked up at the dragon and smiled. "There is much to catch everyone up on."

Inea relaxed and, tucking her wings, shifted to her human form. The fighting was over. Elves and lycan were moving away from one another, but no one was fighting.

"A great deal I'd say." Helena called out as she moved in to attend to her mate. Kieran might be an ass, but he was her's. He would answer for what he did at a better time and place.

Eva settled against Devon. Gareth took Inea to his side. Argoth and Derek joined them. Senias was still in his dragon form, his head beside Devon and Eva and his body curled as if protecting their backs.

Helena turned to Tasha and cleared her throat to get Kieran's attention as well. "When we get back, you'll return to your duties at the palace. We'll discuss everything else once we get there."

"Yes ma'am." Tasha bowed.

"Argoth, you and Derek help Kieran, and let's get him home. We don't need to use our dragon friends for that." Helena moved back to give them space.

"I don't need yer help," Kieran groused, even as he groaned in pain.

"I don't care what you want right now. You'll do as I say because I'm your mate. Since you're so keen on Pack law, let me remind you that in such cases my word is more important than all others and right now, I don't think anyone here is brave enough to challenge my word. You will let them help you and you will walk between them or get in a damned wagon if I have to put you there myself." Helena stood before her mate in a regal pose as the others helped him up.

Devon was proud of his mama and of himself and Senias. As he held Eva in one arm, he moved his hand over the dragon's face with the other to keep him calm. He took the angry glare from his father in stride. He wasn't sure what had happened, but he figured they all had time to find out.

CHAPTER TWENTY-FIVE

COMPROMISE

IT HAD BEEN A few days. The world had calmed down around the packlands. Argoth watched from the side railing as his son, Derek, worked on shifting stances with their new resident, Rory. The young orphan needed the training and the encouragement after all he had been through.

"He's a natural mentor, that one," Kieran's voice caught him off guard. The old scout was still very cautious around the Alpha since their recent confrontations. But life went on, right?

"He is. He'll make a good papa one day. You know, when he stops his prowling." Argoth watched as Kieran placed his hands on the railing close to him. "This don't seem like a social moment. Am I about ta be packless again?"

Kieran's upper body and a good portion of his neck were still healing. Perhaps that was why he couldn't fight anymore. A burn was one thing, but a burn from magical dragon fire stuck around, even on lycan. It was also a reminder to both of what extraordinary power their dragon comrades were capable of and why they truly had to go back to their home world.

"Seen Helena?" Kieran asked.

"No. Not since she took you to the shaman. Why?"

"I asked her here, too." Kieran turned when he heard the door from the side hall close behind them. Their mate stepped through and paused only momentarily at the sight of both men before continuing to them.

"You should still be in bed, letting that heal." She chastised Kieran because that was one thing that she was very good at. That, and she actually did care.

"I wanted to talk to ya both so I wouldn't be repeating myself and there wouldn't be any misunderstandings." Kieran looked between them.

Argoth took a deep breath, and his gaze met Helena's. They both gave Kieran their full attention.

"What I said? What we almost lost? I aim ta make sure things don't happen like that again. Our personal business is our personal business. You'll not be hearing of me having anybody outside of the one I have. Tasha's trustworthy. She has access here without question. And I know you both'll be discreet. We can work toward changing things as soon as it won't be an issue for the packs."

"You're serious?" Argoth's eyes were wide.

"Why?" Helena asked.

"Why not?" Kieran shook his head. "What are ya askin', Hel?"

"Why the sudden shift and change? It isn't like you at all, Kieran Weylyn. In all our years together, you have never compromised. It's always been your way. The only thing that you didn't get your way was when I took you to bed and when I had the pups."

"I never...I never thought about how things affected other people. How my actions affect people I care about? That was until the dragon shoved it in my face. And even then, I fought it. I fought the idea that I was being selfish. I had it in my head that I was the victim of everybody else's selfish ways. Then, while we were fighting over who was what to you, our pups got stolen." He ran his hand through his free hair and sighed.

"Argoth and I - we've fought side by side all these years and I never saw him as anything but a rival and a cheat, when he's been a friend. I was so caught up in my angry world that I didn't give you credit, and I didn't give him credit and I refused ta see my own faults. But since almost being roasted by a creature that fuckin' warned me he might lose control; it woke me up. And I've been thinking back over it all." He took a deep breath and grimaced as the wrap on his burn scraped over it. "So long as we can be discreet, I want us ta live better lives. Once the kids all have their places in life and Argoth's pack has come together, then we can see about changing the rules. Not just for us, but for everybody. First thing, I want ta stop this traditional matchmaking bullshit. And you can be free, and no one can shame you or harm you for your choices."

"We've always been discreet, Kieran. But that's not the point, I suppose." She stood between both men right then and she turned to look at her recognized mate. "I never hoped to hurt you. I pray to the Goddess that you find your true soul mate someday, and I'm sure she will be just as fierce of heart and nature that you are so that you have this too."

Kieran looked back and forth between Argoth and Helena. He felt a lump in his throat, and he wanted to reach out to her and thank her. But he kept his hands to himself and slowly nodded, before walking away to go back to his bedroom, which had become an infirmary and not just a prison. As he turned the corner, he nearly tripped over a petite woman in blue velvet.

"Oh, Lord Kieran! Sorry. I didn't mean to trip you up," Argoth's mate, Leia, quickly got to the side of the hallway, but grabbed the larger man's arm to steady him. The brown tattoos on her muscular hands marked her as the leader of her own pack, even though they were under the protection of Pack Weylyn. Her tanned skin and her eyes were full of mischief as she smiled at him. "Good to see you doing better, Alpha. Have you seen my mate?"

"He's out there watching Derek. Be aware, Helena's out there, too. I just finished talking to 'em both." He didn't feel like getting them into trouble.

"Aren't they always together?" she whispered.

"Have a good one." He continued onward while Leia watched him. Right now, Kieran Weylyn just wanted peace.

"I KNOW WHAT YOU'RE trying to do, and it won't work." Senias finished writing his letter. The ink on the paper was drying now. He looked over at Gareth, who had just come in from... somewhere. The young man was trying his damnedest to impress Inea enough to keep her in this world or make her want to come back. The fool was wearing himself out for his trouble.

Brushing his braids back, Gareth lifted a brow towards the dragon. "Ya don't know that for sure. Inea obviously felt something for me. She practically begged me not to be mad at her and to spend the evening with her. She even asked me ta go with her. This is my home, and she can make it her home. I don't give up easily."

"We're leaving tonight. If you're not willing to leave your home, I suggest you say your goodbyes. You can either pine away for her and wait for her to visit again, this time probably with her kindred. Or you can move on. Up to you." Senias looked over the letter he was leaving for Devon.

"We dragons are not the type to give our heart to one person. We can for a time, but we'll always have mates and other kindred, even if they're friends and not lovers. Singularity is not in our nature. Even if she remained with you, she's still my mate. We may yet have a kitling someday. Would you have an issue with that?"

"I..." Gareth wasn't sure how to answer that.

"Inea keeps multiple kindred. Not all of them are lovers. Seamus is a lover and one that has lasted through time and remained in her heart. But she's had others along with him, Gareth. She'd have you if you'd go with us."

Gareth's blue eyes hardened and narrowed towards Sen.

"Ya keep saying not all lycan fit the mold, well I bet ya not all dragons do either. Time changes everyone." Gareth's fingers flexed as his agitation went up a few notches. "If she leaves, it ain't gonna go how she thinks it will. She's gonna regret leaving and so will you."

"She loves you. I won't argue with the rest." Senias lifted the letter and began folding it.

Gareth watched the dragon and gave a slow shake of his head. "I love her too, but I can't go there now or ever. My home is here and if she wants me, this will have to be her world, too."

"For what it's worth, I like you, Gareth. Don't be like your old man." The dragon got up from the table and moved to go out and find the best place to leave his note. He knew Devon would be gone with Eva for a few more days, at least. He didn't want to interrupt their time.

There was a sound of disgust from the young man. "I'll never be like him... ever." Gareth turned to walk off.

"I hope you're right," Senias muttered under his breath.

CHAPTER TWENTY-SIX

FULL MOON MATES

AFTER EVERYTHING THAT HAD happened, Eva and Devon were finally in their little cabin by themselves. They had earned their time together to bond. They had come through a lot more than most mates had by the time they had come here.

Devon was being undressed by his mate, and his breath was already panting. Eva was against him, lifting the half-shirt she wore upward. His hands took it the rest of the way over her head. Before he could do more, his mate untied his breeches and pulled them down. As she did so, she squatted, took his length in her hands, and began licking the top. She probably made note of his hands, each hitting the sides of the small door frame between the living area and the bedroom when she did it.

It was a good thing he'd built this small cabin to last! Devon heard the wood groan beneath his grip as Eva's mouth worked on him. He watched her and couldn't believe how erotic this was. In all his life, and that had been nearly 50 years now, he'd never felt this turned on.

Eva moved lower to place his cock between her breasts, so that the veined underside slid against her body. Each time he moved it upward, she would reward his patience with a kiss or a lick at the knob's end. Not that he needed the reward, but his mate knew exactly how sexy she must look.

There was that rumble again, only this time it seemed deeper and more feral as Devon's whole body tightened up. "Mmmm... Eva." Her name left his lips as a growling purr of a rumble.

She was getting him good and ready, and her own body was fast becoming wet beneath. All he had to do was let her know. Eva wouldn't let their true mating be while running in the forest where it could go out of control. She wanted him to take her like the prince he was. She wanted that first.

"Enough love." Devon buried his hand in Eva's hair to ease her body away before she made him spill. Reaching down, Devon plucked his mate from the floor and carried her to the bed of pelts and furs. She licked her lips, and her heated gaze wore on his soul. Still grinning in that wolfish way of his, he reached down to grab Eva by the thighs and flipped her to her belly.

Devon pulled Eva to her knees. He tugged and stripped away the skirts, leaving his beauty in nothing but the thin golden belly chain. Leaning down, the big feral ran his tongue from her front to her back, licking the slick wet folds to taste Eva. He couldn't help the growl any more than she could help the needy whine. Their inner wolves were hungry for their mates, and it was showing.

He nudged Eva's legs farther apart and one of his hands moved from her hip to her spine. Calloused fingertips moved up the straight line of muscle and bone and he pushed down in the center of her shoulder blades so Eva's body would lower in the front, tilting her ass up and in the process presenting her dripping wet center to him.

Devon growled deeply as her scent hit him. He couldn't go any longer without being joined with Eva. One hand rubbed the head of his cock against her folds, getting it nice and slick. He pressed into Eva slowly, but without stopping, and it was like their first time together all over again. He tried going slow so as not to hurt his mate, but she was having none of that! His mate pushed back on each thrust.

Buried, Devon leaned over Eva's back to kiss her over one shoulder. First, the movements were with Eva, but then Devon switched it up and was thrusting against her, so their bodies were pounding into one another. Eva was crying out but hadn't reached that perfect spot yet. And as lycan, Devon knew what would get them both there. Without slowing or stopping anything, he brushed Eva's hair away from one side of her neck and shoulder to lay the area bare for him. With a very possessive growl, he bit down on his mate's shoulder. Devon's teeth barely broke skin, but their souls recognized the mark. He had finally fully claimed Eva as his mate.

EVA GROWLED AND SNARLED and howled as she came, not once but several times under the pressure and the persistence of Devon's thrusts. She squirmed and tried to get away once the sensation was becoming difficult to bear, but his bite held her in place. She wasn't sure what to think. For once, she didn't want it to stop, and yet the sensation was almost too much of a good thing. He picked up pace in his thrusts and she heard him growl, "Mine..."

"Mine..." she answered him in return. She might not have teeth in him yet, but that didn't mean a damn thing. Devon was as much hers as she was his. And she'd dare anybody to come between them from this point on. The maddening sensations of pleasure were there to drive her to her lupine form. She was glad she had prepared for this part. Her body shifted. This was part of it. To anyone outside the lycan world, it may have seemed to be a struggle. However, this mating was part of what they were.

She needed to push to get her other side to come forward and he now could also shift and fully take her. Eva was so warm and so happy when she felt herself changing, and with that change, the sensations grew and built once again. His bite dripped blood on the covers beneath them, but she didn't care. She withstood everything with new vigor and pushed back on his thrusting. Her body - new and stronger with the change began pulling on him as he retreated.

This time, when she climaxed, she felt him press hard into her and just stop. His body's thrusting stopped, but she could feel him pulsing deep inside of her. She found an extra level of pleasure at that moment. They both howled at the same time.

It was after the howl and in a moment of coming down from that high that she felt the pain jolt her heavily. She whined, for she couldn't find her human voice right then. Devon immediately backed off and, lying down in his hybrid form, pulled her to him. He rumbled deep in his chest for her.

The familiarity, the scent, the way he touched her, his sounds, and finally, when she came back to it - his aura... they all calmed her. This was their time to bond and fully accept one another. His enormous hands slid up her arms and back down to soothe her. His chest vibrated with that low, deep, and steady rumbling of his. Those calloused fingers smoothed over her back without closing Eva in. If she wanted to move, she could. He wouldn't force his mate.

"Didn't mean to hurt ya." His face moved against her hair and breathed in her scent through the wolf-like muzzle that was his nose right now.

Eva was letting her breath catch up and her heart was calm. She rose to look him over. His body was lightly furred, and his face had the sharp angles of the wolf down to an elongated muzzle, sharp canines, and the pointed lengths of his ears. He was taller, thicker, and broader in this form. Even his animalistic legs were covered in caramel-colored fur with black bands through it. His arms were the same way. His fingers now had sharp claws instead of nail beds.

She wondered if she looked the same. So, she allowed herself to shift back to her human form.

Eva moved her hands over his face, his snout, and his teeth. Those were what had marked her. Then she leaned down and kissed him in the most sensitive place there, his nose showing him that this was just as handsome to her as the more human form. He slowly shifted while she watched.

"You healed, love?" he asked, a hand moving over her arm and shoulder gently.

"Yes," she whispered, before cuddling up with him. Devon rumbled and held her. They had over a week yet together and alone. There was no rush to enjoy one another to exhaustion beyond this, though both had a feeling it might just happen over and over again.

Chapter Twenty-Seven

SAYING GOODBYE

Devon,

What else is there for me to say, than I love you as a friend close to my heart? You have proven to me that loyalty and faith are yet alive. That there are people out there who can see us as more than tools or objects to be ordered around and used.

Alas, as we spoke of before your mating, I can no longer remain in this world to enjoy your company and the company of your mate and hopefully your many pups as they get here. I believe what I did to your father is proof enough of that. But I hope to visit at some point and see the dual moons yet again. Many blessings upon you and yours.

Senias of Morias

SATISFIED WITH THE FINAL reading, the dragon tied the letter with a piece of twine and placed it in Devon's room, where he knew the man would find it. He looked around one last time as he strolled through the castle, greeting people and bidding them farewell. By the time he got back to the room that Inea had used all this time of their stay, he could hear Gareth's voice. Sighing, he leaned against the hallway wall and watched from outside.

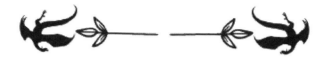

"So he's right, yer still leaving? Even though I love ya and I know ya love me, too - no matter what bullshit ya spout at me otherwise."

"I'm sorry." Inea broke. She'd been doing so well. But hearing his voice and feeling how upset he was? She took a deep breath and continued to pack her bag.

Stepping to the dragoness, Gareth took her by the upper arms so that she couldn't turn away.

"Look me in the eyes and tell me that ya don't love me enough to stay. Tell me, Inea! Look right at me and tell me that yer gonna go through that portal for another man!" The ache was there in his words. It felt like a betrayal.

"He's not just another man, Gar! I love him as I love you, but I've loved him and he's loved me for centuries! I can't ignore my feelings for him any more than I can ignore my feelings for you. Do you think I'm just going to forget anything about you and pretend this didn't happen? Do you think this is easy for me? I want you to come with me. Please, Gar."

"Don't go, Inea. Stay here and be my mate. I'll give ya the world if ya just stay. We can see this entire world together." He had let go of her arms and took her hands to lift and press his lips to her knuckles. "I'm begging."

"Your world, Gar, not mine. And it's making me turn on myself. I'm losing myself to this world's magic." Inea whispered. "Sen and I can't stay for so many years. I don't know how the others do it, but we can't stay." She shook her head. "I would take you with me in an instant, but I can't stay here."

"Then ask the others how they do it. Find a way!" Gareth huffed roughly and looked away for a moment. "You already know I have no desire to cross the portals to a world in which our kind hide away from humans or face death. Supernaturals are far superior to humans and yet in that world, the weaker race rules? No, thank ya. I'll not hide who and what I am. Living in the shadows of others and in fear of being seen? No, that's no life if ya ask me."

"You've already said you won't go. I understand. We're at an impasse." She jerked his hands down to force their bodies together, and she let go to hug him. Her fingers spread into his hair, and she kissed him for the last time. ~ Live your life. Do not ache for me. ~ She pushed the enchantment she had prepared into his mind. She didn't want him to dwell on her and pine away for her. If he would not come with her, then he deserved to live his life to its fullest and give other women a chance.

Gareth felt the euphoria of magic. Instantly he realized what she was doing, and he fought to get away. "No. Don't..." Gareth actually snarled at her. He stepped back and shook his head as if to rid it of her magic. His eyes squeezed shut, and he growled as one hand reached up to shove his fingers through his hair.

"I can take it away. It won't hurt..."

Gareth looked back at Inea sharply, his pupils dilated, and his nose was flaring as he breathed deeply, "Nah, ya don't get to do that to us, woman. Yer leaving, then ya do it with me in yer head and yer heart, just as ya leave part of yerself in mine. We can be fuckin' miserable together in two worlds."

Tears streamed from her eyes, the oblong pupils showing as she struggled to keep her own under control. "I don't want you to hurt. Don't you get that?"

"And I don't want ta forget you!"

Either path she took would hurt him. Rock, meet hard place. So, she'd let him have it his way. If he wanted to suffer with her instead of moving on in ignorant bliss, that was on him.

"I can't stay." She picked up her bag and pulled it over her shoulder and head. "If you're staying here, I hope to come back to see you someday. I don't know when. If you don't go with me now, I cannot guarantee how you could find me if you ever do come to the other world."

His pained expression said it all. But he added one more thing, along with his own tears. "I could find ya no matter where ya were, Flutters."

Inea turned to walk out of the room, and seeing her dragon mate waiting, a bit of relief passed over her features. But that was short-lived. Catching up with Inea just as she reached Senias, Gareth got in front of her and stood facing her with the dragon right behind him. Both hands cupped his woman's beautiful face as they stared eye to eye for a moment. ~ I don't care about them, Inea. You are taking part of me with you. I love you, and that will not change. ~ Gareth caught Inea's mouth in a deep, passionate kiss that went on until they were both breathless. He then backed away to shift forms and ran for the woods.

Senias rushed the next few steps to her and held her in his arms. She was sobbing, and he understood. He leaned down to pick up her bag, as he already had his own. They walked out of the castle proper. Turning, he pushed portal magic forward into a circular blue vortex.

At the top of a nearby hill, Gareth threw his head back and gave a low-keening howl.

The dragons stepped through the small portal and instantly out of the packlands.

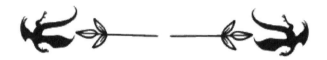

THE PORTAL HE HAD cast let them out into the beautiful gardens surrounding the massive world portal in the draconic city-state of Iona. They could hear people scuffling around the place and see the glow of the building-sized portal only some leagues away.

"Crimson runs the portal. Their guards are walking around, and their customs officials are busy with the flow of traffic in and out. However, security is apathetic at best these days. Lord Rashgun of Iona tells me if we have any trouble with the credentials he has provided to us, do not allow them to take us into custody. Come to him in his palace. Understand the plans?"

Senias began handing her the documents the dragon lord had provided to them. "Our new identities. Enya Kaltan and Jean-Michel Raudine. Hmmm...interesting names."

Senias moved Inea to a bench nearby. He helped her, held her, and watched over her.

"Get hold of yourself. Get your breath and we can wait." Senias sighed.

"I'm sorry," she whispered. "I tried."

"Don't apologize, dear. You've got five times the heart I have. Of course, you fell in love. The kid's adorable. And that psychotic touch to his eyes? Damn." He tried humor at first, of course. He wasn't sure what else to do.

"Sen..."

"Yeah, I'll be quiet now." Senias swallowed. "Time to go back home."

REVIEWS ARE SO IMPORTANT! Especially to indie authors, like me, who are trying to bring you more stories in a timely manner and with the best possible tools and quality we can afford. When you write a review, no matter how small, it can boost my sales by encouraging more readers to try the book, help the books get included in special promotions run by platforms, and help the ranking of the books. Also, consider this—I am a small business trying to make it, and I hire other small business owners along the way. None of us are CEOs of mega corporate publishing companies. And when we make sales and get reviews, we do a little dance and celebrate!

More than that, reviews let me know someone out there wanted to read my stories. It drives me and my coauthor to keep going and improve our skills. Reviews tell me that our characters actually affected someone well enough that they wrote about them and the experience we provided for them as an audience. I hope you understand the magnitude of how important your review is to me. Thank you!

Want to leave a review? Look for me as Rachel D. Adams on Goodreads and BookBub. Recommend my books there. Or, if you want to focus on the platform you prefer, all of my books and the links are here:

linktr.ee/rachdadams

Want to keep reading about the adventures of our characters?
Sign up for the newsletter or find the future urban fantasy & para-
normal romance series.
Everything is available on my website:

racheldadams.com

35721583R00102